THE AVENUE

THE AVENUE

Cecil Allen

First published in 2022

Copyright © 2022 Cecil Allen

E-mail: cecilallen93seapark@gmail.com
The moral right of Cecil Allen to be identified as the author
of the work has been asserted in accordance with the
Copyright, Designs and patents Act of 1988
Paperback ISBN:

Cover design by Brendan Bierne
Cover painting by Godfrey Smeaton

ABOUT THE AUTHOR

The award winning writer Cecil Allen is the grandson of the famous actor and writer Ira Allen. Cecil is the author of the hugely popular novels '*The Actor*' and '*Constructing Alice.*' He is a retired college lecturer from the Dublin Institute of Technology and holds a BA from Indiana University and an MFA from the University of Minnesota. He was a broadcaster with RTE for over twenty years and represented Ireland twice at International Toastmasters Competitions.

He is the father of two sons and lives in Malahide with his wife Julie.

For Molly and Maeve

'Life can only be understood backwards; but it must be lived forwards.'

Søren Kierkegaard (1813-1855)

TABLE OF CONTENTS

INTRODUCTION

The year is 1950 and the Second World War, or *The Emergency* as it was known in Ireland, is over, food rationing is nearly finished, non-military products are being manufactured and the word teenager has just been invented.

The Avenue is on the north side of Dublin. There are nineteen identical yellow-brick terraced houses on one side and twenty on the other, all owned by landlords and rented on a long-term basis.

Each has a front parlour and a combined living room/dining room from where a staircase leads to two upstairs bedrooms. Opposite the staircase in the living room is a fireplace with a nar-row metal mantelpiece, which is usually home to the family clock, or a statue of the Sacred Heart or the Virgin Mary. This family room is usually colourfully wallpapered and along the top of the wallpaper is a thick border-frieze of pale flowers.

The kitchen, which many of the people refer to as the scullery, is an extension that juts out from the back of the house. Most fea-ture a gas stove, a few wooden presses and a sink with a drainer. Over the sink is a little-used gas water heater.

Yet apart from all these similarities, each house is a world of its own and as different from the next as the people who live there.

For the most part, this street is quiet and a good place to raise children. Nearly all of the youngsters who live there were born there or in one of the nearby nursing homes on the Glasnevin Road. When they are old enough, they go to one of the two local schools, which unsurprisingly are both named St. Mary's. They make their Holy Communion and Confirmation then leave, get a job if they can, marry, have children, live their life and then pass on. Some of them do it without ever leaving The Avenue where they were born and reared.

The people on the Avenue are decent hard-working people. Some are happy, some troubled and a few are desperate. In the 1950s there were many things not openly talked about, though in reality there were few secrets.

Most of these stories begin and end in the year 1950, a few take place before 1950 and a few take place beyond that year.

The first story *Mrs Green's Money* begins on 1st January, 1950. It's the beginning of a new day, a new year and a new decade. The sky is still dark and a cold north wind is blowing.

CHAPTER 1

MRS GREEN'S MONEY

Most people liked Mrs Green.

She was a big woman with shiny silver hair that made her look regal, and fat arms that made her look imposing. She was also paralysed from the waist down, and as long as anyone could remember she had been bedridden. Some people thought she had been injured in an accident; others that she had been struck down by a mysterious illness. No one really knew and Mrs Green never talked about herself or her health.

Mr Green had positioned his wife's bed by the window in the front parlour, so she could take part in the life of the Avenue. Every morning at ten, except when it was raining, Mrs Green opened her window and when anyone approached she stopped them and involved them in conversation. It didn't matter if it was an adult or a child, Mrs Green always wanted to talk. Every birth, every death, every visitor to the Avenue, every incident, minor or major was of great interest to her. Sometimes for fun, or simply to avoid talking to her, the children would crawl under her window and emerge unseen on the other side. Sometimes as they crawled they would hear Mrs Green having difficulty breathing, then she would start to cough, and teasing her wasn't fun anymore.

Across the Avenue from Mrs Green lived the unruly, boisterous Farrell family. Their home was filled with music, laughter and talk. Mr Farrell loved football and in his youth he had been asked to try out for Bohemians, the local football team; he was never invited to play for them but he took great pride in having trained with his heroes. Every Friday evening before tea, Mr Farrell, his ten-year-old son Johnny and his six-year-old daughter Molly had a family football kick-about on the Avenue. The game would come to an abrupt end when Mrs Farrell called her husband and children for their tea.

Mrs Farrell was another large woman, who played the piano for her own entertainment and the entertainment of her husband and children. She also believed every imaginable superstition. When baking soda bread she scored the crust with a cross so that the devil would not be trapped in the loaf. She believed anyone who killed a robin would have life-long bad luck. Her darkest belief was if you counted the number of cars following a hearse, that was the number of years you had left to live. She also insisted the Avenue was located in Glasnevin. It wasn't, it was in Phibsboro, which was a little less posh. When her children wanted to tease her, they would chat loudly about how they liked living in Phibsboro.

Many a day, young Johnny Farrell would open the front door of his house and look across the Avenue; if there wasn't someone standing at Mrs Green's open window he'd run across and have a chat with her. After talking to her he always felt a little better. Although she never said it, he knew he was her favourite.

Mrs Green loved to watch the children playing. One day when they had finished their game of rounders, she beckoned young Johnny to her window.

'Yes, Mrs Green?' he said, his eyes just about reaching the window ledge.

'Stand back from the window so I can see you.'

Johnny did as instructed.

'That's better. I have something to ask you. Would you like to be my messenger?'

He nodded his agreement, not knowing what a messenger was.

Mrs Green cocked her head to one side. 'You don't know what a messenger is, do you?'

Johnny shook his head.

'You should always ask when you don't understand something. That's how you learn new things. Now, do you have something to ask me?'

He thought for a moment. 'What does a messenger do?'

'Good question. A messenger is someone who delivers messages from one place to another. Now would you like to be my messenger?'

'Yes,' he said.

'Good, I'll let Mr Moore know.'

So Johnny became Mrs Green's messenger and his job was to go to Moore's corner grocery shop and get whatever Mrs Green needed; a quarter pound of Donnelly's sausages, four ounces of hard cheese, a pound of loose sugar and occasionally a naggin of whiskey. He was never given money to pay for the purchases, everything went on the slate. When he returned with the messages he placed them on the window ledge and Mrs Green moved them on to her bed.

For this great service, Johnny received sixpence per week. However, there was one stipulation; he had to tell Mrs Green what he purchased with the money. Sixpence was a lot of money for a little boy. He could go to the cinema and treat himself to four mounds of Cleeves toffee; he could buy a slingshot, or a comic book or even a bag of marbles. A huge sixpenny wafer of ice cream was also an option as was a bottle of Taylor Keith's red lemonade. Once, Johnny saved two weeks' money and bought a potato gun.

Every Saturday morning, he stood in front of Mrs Green's open window and told her what he had bought or what he planned to buy with his sixpence. She would nod her head and smile, and sometimes she would laugh and that would make him laugh as well.

The day he told Mrs Green about the rubber worms was a day like no other. Johnny bought them in a joke shop and when his father wasn't looking he slipped the worms into his father's sandwich. Just as his father was about to bite into the sandwich he saw the worms, jumped and shouted words Johnny hadn't heard before. New words, strange words and when he repeated the words to Mrs Green she laughed so heartily her body shook and the bed rattled. The rattling bed made Johnny giggle and his giggling made Mrs Green laugh until she snorted. The more she snorted the more Johnny giggled and they snorted and giggled and laughed until they ached.

Many a time after that Mrs Green said to Johnny, 'Tell me again about the rubber worms and don't forget the bit about your father's funny words.' And before Johnny even finished the story the laughing and the giggling would start.

One day Mrs Green asked Johnny to go to the shop to get a quarter pound of broken biscuits. As he walked back the temptation to open the bag and eat one was almost irresistible. He resisted for as long as he could but then, just before he turned the corner into the Avenue, he opened the bag and gobbled a Marietta biscuit. Even as he swallowed the dry crumbs he felt awful.

He ran to Mrs Green's window, plonked the bag on the ledge and was about to run away when she called, 'Wait a minute.'

He stopped. Mrs Green looked at the bag then looked at him. *How did she know he had eaten a biscuit? Could she read his mind?*

Mrs Green opened the bag, rummaged around in it, found a chocolate biscuit and handed it to him.

'That's for being a good boy,' she said and as he took the beautiful chocolate-covered biscuit, he felt even more terrible.

One day, he was in the middle of telling Mrs Green one of his adventures when she said, 'Why don't you tell me the rest of the story tomorrow. I'm a little tired today.' Then she reached up and pulled down the window. She began to close the window more and more often, and some days the window did not open at all. Then a whole week went by with the window shut. Then Johnny saw something he had never seen before at Mrs Green's window: dark curtains. There was a white card with a black border pinned to the hall door. Neighbours and strangers went in and out of Mrs Green's house and Johnny's father and mother sat him down and explained that Mrs Green had died.

'She's with God now,' Mrs Farrell said and blessed herself. 'Why don't we say a prayer for her?'

For a long time, Johnny missed Mrs Green's money. He used to think of all the things he could have bought and all the things he could have done with Mrs Green's money. He remembered how she loved to hear about the things he bought and the things he did with her money; he remembered her happy face and her laughter and he knew it wasn't Mrs Green's money he missed, it was Mrs Green.

CHAPTER 2

PILLOWS

Mrs Bridy Flynn was an intelligent and proud Cork woman who had lived longer in Dublin than she had in her native Cork. The 'culchies' or the 'boggers', as some of the Avenue's children unkindly called the Flynns, were quiet people who, as Mrs Quinn use to say, 'kept to themselves' meaning they were a bit stand-offish. Mrs Flynn was a small soft-spoken woman who seldom raised her voice and always kept her own counsel. Eamon Flynn, Bridy's husband was a big man with great bushy eyebrows and a well-groomed beard who enjoyed playing the fiddle in his céilí band the Shandon Shamrocks. Anne, their pretty sixteen-year-old daughter, completed the Flynn family.

Eamon worked for the Revenue Commissioners and many of his neighbours envied him his good government job and small family. Every morning at eight o'clock he walked to his work in O'Connell Street and every evening at a quarter past six he placed his set of keys on the sideboard in his living room and took his seat by the fire. The Flynn home was a happy home. Early in his marriage, Eamon realised his wife was cleverer than he, so he left all the important thinking to her.

The evening Eamon opened the front door of his home and did not smell the aroma of freshly baked bread he knew something was wrong. Bridy was sitting at an unlit fire in the living room and she shuddered when she saw him. During their eighteen years of marriage, Eamon thought he had seen every expression his wife's face could conjure up, but that evening he saw a new emotion on her face. Dread. He immediately pulled off his tweed cap and went to his wife.

'What is it, love?' he asked taking the chair opposite her. 'What's wrong?'

'It's worse than wrong, Eamon.'

'Take your time and tell me what happened.'

'I went to Moore's to get some groceries and on the way back I stopped and chatted with Mr Green. I knew Mason was due to collect the rent so I didn't stay long. The minute I opened the door of the house I heard crying and Mason's voice in the parlour. I rushed into the room and there was Anne on the sofa sobbing and Mason standing over her buckling the belt of his trousers. "What in God's name is going on?" I asked after I rushed over to Anne.

"It's a little misunderstanding," Mason said. "I'm in a bit of a hurry. You can pay on the double next week."

"What did you do?" I cried, grabbing Mason's sleeve.

"Nothing," he said and jerked his arm free of my grip.

"He hurt me, Mammy," Anne said, sobbing into her hands.

"Get out and never come back," I shouted after him. "I'm putting the police on to you."'

I went to Anne and took her in my arms

'Am I a bad person?' she asked.

'No love. You did nothing wrong. It wasn't your fault.'

Eamon listened to his wife and every time she mentioned Mason's name he wanted to rush out, find the man and pull the skin off his body. But he didn't, he fixed his eyes on his wife's face and listened to every word she said.

When Bridy had finished talking, Eamon went to his daughter's bedroom and took her in his arms. He stroked her hair and told her he loved her and would always be there for her. When he finally left his daughter's room he stepped into the small back garden and sat on the window ledge; his body shuddered and he wept for his child.

Later when Anne had gone to bed, Eamon and Bridy sat on the opposite sides of a dying fire. Head bowed, he listened to his wife re-live over and over the events she witnessed in the parlour. At some point when his wife was talking, he bit his lower lip and tore a tiny sliver of skin off it.

'How could he, she's only a child,' he said as blood oozed from his lip and trickled down his chin. 'I'll kill that fucking man.'

Bridy grabbed her husband's knees.

'You'll do nothing of the sort,' she whispered. 'And keep your voice down.'

'We'll have to bring Anne to the church and have Canon Breathnach bless her. He'll know what to do.'

'Canon Breathnach is the last person on this earth we'll go to. No one must ever be told about this.'

'What about the police?'

'The police will do nothing, our first and last concern is Anne. We have to do what's best for her.'

'And what is that,' asked Eamon and the distressed face of his beautiful daughter flashed into his mind.

Mrs Flynn removed her hands from her husband's knees and placed them on her lap.

'Right now the best thing we can do is nothing.'

Eamon Flynn jolted upright but before he could say a word, Bridy raised her hand and silenced him.

'Mason must never set foot in this house again. Tomorrow you will go to his offices in Dorset Street and make arrangements to pay the rent there every week. I don't want that man in this house ever again.'

'I'll go down to his office alright, but I won't talk to him. I'll kill him, that's what I'll do.'

'That might make you feel better, Eamon, but how would it help Anne? Think man, Mason could throw us out of the house tomorrow and how do you think that would that improve the situation?'

Bridy and Eamon talked long and hard into the night and slowly she convinced him of the wisdom of her thinking. The following day Eamon went to Mason's office and arranged to pay the rent there.

During the next four weeks, Anne changed from being an outgoing happy child into an introverted moody girl. Her mother tried to get her to talk about what happened but all Anne said was 'I don't want to talk about it.' Anne retreated into her childhood, she took a renewed interest in childish games and books, but at night she stayed in her room and cried. The police were not informed.

'I think something is wrong with me, Ma,' Anne said to her mother one morning before she left for school. 'I get sick in the mornings and yesterday I fell asleep in class.'

'There's a cold going around, I'll get a tonic from the chemist and you'll soon be right as rain.'

When Anne went to school Bridy made a cup of tea, sat at the table and a violent chill convulsed her entire body. She knew no tonic would help her daughter's condition. She remembered what happened to young Patricia Ronan; she was a young unmarried girl who found herself pregnant back in Ballygurteen. Bridy remembered the righteous fury on the face of the parish priest as he pounded on the front door of the Ronan family farm. She remembered seeing the priest pull the poor girl screaming from her house. She remembered the two nuns stepping out of a black car and taking hold of the girl. She remembered the girl pleading for help and the shocked look on the faces of the girl's parents as the two nuns bundled their daughter into the back of the car.

When Eamon returned from work he saw the look on his wife's face and he knew something was terribly wrong; he said nothing. He waited patiently and when Anne was in bed he asked Bridy to tell him what was bothering her.

'It's a lot more than bothering me, Eamon.' Bridy looked off into the distance and tears moistened her eyes. 'Anne is pregnant.'

'Jesus Christ, are you sure?'

'I'm as sure as I can be.'

'We should have talked with Canon Breathnach. Bridy, he's a man of God.'

'He may be a man of God, but he's the man who would put your beautiful daughter in a Magdalene Laundry and worse put our grandchild in an orphanage to be sold.'

'You're talking rubbish.'

'You have a short memory, man. Have you forgotten young Patricia Ronan from Ballygurteen who got herself pregnant? Do you want that to happen to our Anne?'

'No I don't, but what can we do, the child will be illegitimate?' Eamon said, staring into his wife's face.

'Children are not legitimate or illegitimate, children are children.'

'What about the shame of it.'

'Anne did nothing to be ashamed of and neither did our grandchild, so I'll hear no more talk of shame.'

Eamon sat uncomfortably in his chair. 'What are we going to do when the priest comes knocking on our door?'

'I have an idea.'

Bridy told Eamon her idea and they talked well into the small hours of the morning and before they went to bed they had devised their plan.

After six weeks of morning sickness the Flynn household returned to normal. During the summer Bridy took Anne to stay with her sister Maureen and her husband Paul on her farm on the outskirts of Ballygurteen. They arranged that Anne would stay on the farm until the child was born and then return to the Avenue.

The day after her daughter went to Cork, Bridy stopped at Mrs Green's window and during their little chat Bridy told Mrs Green, in the strictest of confidence, that she was pregnant.

'Oh, wonderful! I thought you were looking well and if you don't mind me saying it, I think you're beginning to show a little. Congratulations, I'm sure young Anne will be a great help to you.'

'My sister Maureen hurt her leg in a farm accident and Anne is down there with her helping look after the children,' said Bridy, lying ever so sweetly.

'Your sister is fortunate to have such a good helper. I'll say a prayer for her and congratulations again, Bridy.'

Bridy nodded shyly and as she walked home she smiled to herself content in the knowledge that by the end of the day every woman on the Avenue would know about her pregnancy and her poor sister's accident.

For the next few days, neighbours and friends congratulated Mrs Flynn on her good news.

'Aren't you lucky, a new child at your age,' said the begrudging Mrs Delaney. 'Do you think you'll be up to it? I mean at your age.'

'Of course, I'll be up to it, lots of women my age have babies,' replied Bridy.

'You'll need plenty of rest,' said Mrs Delaney. 'Make that big man of yours do some of the housework. That will learn him, life's not all pleasure.'

When Eamon joined the Shandon Shamrocks for their weekly session he received great congratulations, lots of back slaps and more than a few free pints.

About that time Bridy visited Guiney's Drapery Shop in Talbot St and bought four different sized pillows. On the day Anne was five months pregnant Bridy placed the smallest of the pillows under her dress and each month she replaced it with a larger one.

〰〰〰

The day Father Price, the curate in Ballygurteen, visited her sister's farm was a nerve-racking day. The jolly, chubby priest ate a plate of fruit cake and drank a large glass of buttermilk, but when the food and drink were consumed his face fell serious and he inquired about the pregnant girl that had been seen about the farm.

Maureen took a deep breath and delivered her prepared answer.

'It's sensitive, Father, and I know I can count on your discretion,' she said in a hushed voice. 'The girl is my niece, my sister's daughter. Now didn't the silly young girl go and marry a British soldier. The people in Dublin are up in arms. Father, I'm relying on you not to breathe a word.' Maureen tapped the side of her nose conspiratorially. 'The child will be baptised Catholic, no need to worry yourself about that. The child's father may be a British soldier but he's a good Catholic lad from Wales.'

'You can count on my discretion,' the overweight priest said and looked around to see if there was any more cake.

'Would you like another slice of cake?' asked Maureen.

'Well, a little bit wouldn't go astray.'

When he had finished eating his third slice of cake, the priest made his farewell. The portly fellow sat on the saddle of his bicycle and before he pressed down on the pedal he wondered why that woman kept tapping the side of her nose when she spoke.

〰〰〰

The sight of a uniformed telegram boy cycling up the Avenue was unusual. Mrs Green watched for the boy's destination. When he stopped at Number Twenty One she poked her head out the window. The boy knocked on the yellow door and when Bridy opened the door, the boy handed her a small brown envelope. Bridy rooted in the pocket of her apron, found a small coin and handed it to the boy. Once she had closed the hall door she tore open the telegram.

Everyone fine, special guest arriving soon.

Bridy folded the telegram and placed it on the sideboard. She went to her bedroom and removed a pre-packed suitcase from the wardrobe. She took a number 10 bus to O'Connell Street, went into the GPO, phoned her husband and told him she was on her way to Cork. The following day in Ballygurteen, Bridy and Maureen waited anxiously in the living room while the midwife helped Anne give birth in the small back bedroom.

'Congratulations, it's a boy,' the midwife said as she handed the child to the new mother. 'A beautiful boy, he's gorgeous.' Then she pulled open the bedroom door and beckoned the two sisters into the room.

While they were admiring the baby, the midwife pulled a notebook from the pocket of her uniform. 'I need some information for the birth certificate. Mother's maiden name?'

Maureen glanced from Bridy to Anne.

'Bridy O'Brien,' answered Mrs Flynn, without so much as a moment's hesitation.

'Bridy? But I heard you call your daughter "Anne", earlier on?'

'You did, she never liked the name Bridy – did you, Anne? So we call her by her second name.'

'She's right, the name Bridy is a bit old-fashioned, but we have to put the mother's legal name on the birth certificate,' said the midwife. 'So Bridy Anne it has to be, I'm afraid.'

'You're right. What name are you giving the child?' asked the midwife, turning to Anne.

'Sean,' Anne replied, looking at her mother. 'I'd like to call him Sean.'

'Sean's a lovely name,' the midwife said and jotted the name in her notebook.

'And what's the father's name?'

'Eamon Flynn,' replied Bridy.

It was a dark rainy evening and needles of rain flicked into Bridy and Anne's faces when they stepped off the bus at Dargan's chemist shop. It had been a long trip from Ballygurteen and the two women were cold, tired and weary. Carrying baby Sean in her arms, Bridy walked up Blessington St.

'Let me carry my baby,' Anne said to her mother.

'No,' said Bridy sharply. 'To the world, Sean is not your baby, he's my baby and it's best we start now.' Then, as her daughter's face fell, she added more kindly, 'You can hold him all you want when we get home.'

As they reached the Avenue, the inquisitive Miss Catherine Hennessy came flying out of her house to greet them. 'You've had your baby Mrs Flynn, what excitement!' she said. 'Can I have a little look?'

Bridy moved a corner of the blanket, and baby Sean wrinkled his little face at the damp, cold air.

'Baby doesn't like to be disturbed,' said Miss Hennessy, amused. 'What's the child's name?'

'Sean, he's named after his great grandfather,' said Bridy.

'A little boy, oh he's beautiful,' she smiled, then added to Anne, 'It must be lovely to have a new baby brother.'

'It is. We'd better go now, we don't want him to catch a cold.'

Eamon was waiting for them in the living room. He took his grandson in his arms and held him close.

'I made a cot for your little fellow. I didn't know what he was going to be so I painted it yellow, like the hall door, and it looks lovely. It's upstairs in your bedroom.' Eamon gave the baby back to his wife then placed his burly arms around his daughter and murmured, 'Don't worry, love. Everything is going to be fine, just fine.'

And so Sean Flynn joined the residents of the Avenue. He was baptised in St Joseph's Church, Berkley Road and everyone on the Avenue accepted him as just another child.

CHAPTER 3

THE GIRL IN THE BLUE DRESS

Danny Dunne flipped up the lid of his father's Phillips radio-gram and placed the new 78 rpm record he had purchased that afternoon on to the machine. He flicked a switch, the disc plopped onto the turntable, the record player's arm moved across the revolving turntable, dropped onto the disc and with a quiet crackle the big voice of Frankie Laine singing *Ghost Riders in the Sky* filled the room.

'Give us a twirl,' Grainne said to her brother as she took his hand and started to jive. 'Is that your new shirt?'

'Yea.'

'Lovely. Are you going to ask Sandra Wogan to dance tonight?'

'Why would I do that?'

'Because you fancy her.'

Danny looked away.

She laughed. 'Look, I know Sandra, she was in my class, do you want me to introduce you to her or not?'

'Not, and keep your nose out of my business.'

'Will you two stop your dancing and arguing? You nearly knocked the statue of the Blessed Virgin off the mantelpiece,' Mrs Dunne said as she came into the living room.

In the house next door, Shay McBride slid his skinny legs into his new drainpipe trousers and stretched the narrow pants' leg to almost breaking point. He slipped his large feet into his luminous light green socks and slid on his new winklepicker shoes. After he Brylcreamed his hair, he stood tall and admired himself in the mirror.

'Bring on the girls,' he said and winked at himself. He was ready for the hop. Time to collect his friend Danny Dunne from next door.

'What do you think?' Shay asked when Mr Dunne opened the hall door to him.

'What are you wearing? You look like a feckin eejit.'

'If you say that Mr Dunne, I must look cool.'

'Mary, will you look at the state of Shay, he looks like an upside-down traffic light.'

Shay swaggered into the living room.

'Ah leave him alone. You look lovely Shay,' said Mrs Dunne.

'Thank you, Mrs Dunne, you're a woman of great taste.'

'Ah, get away with yourself.'

'Are you ready Danny? Don't want to give Jarlath Hacket a chance to get your girl,' Shay said, looking in the mirror and pulling a comb through his hair.

'Danny, I didn't know you have a girl?' Mrs Dunne said with a bright sparkle in her eye. 'Who is she? Do I know her mother?'

'Ma, I don't have a girl. Shay, keep your mouth shut.'

'Sorry, Mrs Dunne he doesn't have a girl. He never had a girl and the way things are going he never will get a girl.'

'Shut up Shay.'

'My lips are sealed.'

'Let's go,' Danny said, as he pushed his friend towards the front door.

'Danny, wait,' Mr Dunne said and slipped five shillings into his son's hand. 'It will get you into the hop and buy a bag of chips on the way home.'

'Thanks Da,' Danny said and quickly pocketed the money.

'I bet you were a cool kid when you were our age, Mr Dunne,' Shay said.

'I've had my day and Shay, I take it back about your downpipes, they look "cool".'

'Drainpipes not downpipes. Mr Dunne, maybe you're the one that's not cool.'

'Get out of here,' Mr Dunne said and laughed out loud.

━━┿╍┿━━

The first person Danny and Shay saw when they arrived at the Scouts Hall was Jarlath Hacket. The tall, blond, extremely confident Hacket was near the top of the queue and he and his friends were laughing and flirting with the girls in front of them.

'Your man Hacket is good-looking alright but he's full of himself,' Grainne said, joining them in the queue.

Danny and Shay shrugged and swaggered into the crowded noisy hall. The far side of the hall was awash with teenage girls; some were in full swing skirts worn over layers of fluffy crinolines and others wore straight, long pencil skirts in an array of colours and patterns. Most girls wore white bobby socks, saddle shoes or ballerina flats. The opposite side of the hall was lined with teenage boys wearing patterned, plaid, check or corduroy sports coats with mismatched pants. Most were wearing narrow ties and brown leather or suede shoes. The velvet voice of Nat King Cole crooning *Unforgettable* belted from the huge speakers on the stage.

'Is your mot here?' Shay asked, stretching his neck to look around the hall.

'She's not my mot.'

'There's Mich and Tony,' said Shay and took off.

Danny leaned against the wall and, pretending he was bored, looked around the hall. In the mineral bar at the end of the hall sat Jarlath Hacket and his friends. In the centre of the floor, dancing with each other, was a gaggle of girls; the noise of their laughing and gossiping nearly drowned out Nat King Cole's voice. When Danny's eyes found the girl in the blue dress the rush of delight and confusion he experienced nearly took his breath away. It was the same dress she had worn the first night he saw her, three weeks ago. Tonight, Sandra had added a white neck scarf and a white cardigan draped around her shoulders. Danny thought the additions made her look ever prettier.

As he stood thinking about how he would ask her to dance, Jarlath Hacket tapped him on the shoulder.

'How are ya, Danny? Heard you had a thing for Sandra.'

'I don't know what you're talking about.'

'Your mouthy friend Shay told me to keep away from her, so I figured you must fancy her. Now I ask you, why aren't you dancing with her? I know, Shay told us that too, you're afraid to ask her up. Well, let me show you how it's done.'

Hacket swanned across the hall to the girl in the blue dress.

Shay arrived back at Danny's side. 'I told Hacket to keep away from Sandra,' he said, adjusting his tie.

'I know you did, you feckin eejit. And you told him I fancy her too.'

'What's wrong with that?'

'Now he's decided to ask her to dance, to "show me how it's done".'

'Then you better move fast and get there before he does.'

'He's already there, look.'

The confident Jarlath had positioned himself in front of Sandra and was clearly asking her to dance. Danny tensed. Shay leaned on Danny's shoulder. They waited and when Sandra shook her head, Danny's heart leapt. But Hacket wasn't taking no for an answer. He took her hand and tried to coax her onto the floor. She shook her head again, then whipped her fingers out of his and turned her back on him.

Shay guffawed behind his hand. 'Will you look at that? She told him to sling his hook.'

As Hacket strolled back to his friends trying to look like he hadn't a care in the world, Sandra glanced across the floor and smiled at Danny.

'Did you see that?' Shay asked.

'I did, I did.'

'You're alright there Danny, are you going to ask her up?'

Danny knew his time had come. In the full gaze of Shay and Hacket he set out across the dance floor. He was halfway there when he started to doubt whether he had made the right decision. The closer he got to Sandra, the prettier she got and the more nervous he became. Suddenly he was standing in front of her and she was looking at him.

'May I have this dance?' he asked in a voice he hardly recognised as his own.

Sandra blushed and looked down.

Near panic gripped his heart.

Her eyes slowly came up and met his. 'Sorry, I'm not dancing,' she murmured ever so softly.

Disappointed, embarrassed and mortified he stood frozen to the spot. He wished the floor would open and swallow him whole. He was thinking about the long walk back across the dance floor when his sister took his hand and pulled him onto the floor.

'It's not the end of the world, it just feels like it,' Grainne said as Perry Como's voice belted out *Hot Diggity* around the hall. 'Show her how well you can dance.'

'I don't feel like dancing.'

'You have to dance with me. I don't like the way your friend Hacket is looking at me, I think he fancies me.'

'He's not my friend,' Danny complained, but he started to jive.

When the set was over, Grainne kissed him on the cheek.

'You're still the best dancer in the hall, keep your chin up,' she said and was gone.

Danny, still wounded, returned to the bench on the boys' side of the hall and sat looking at the floor. From nowhere a girl in a yellow swing skirt sat down beside him.

'Hello, you're Danny aren't you?'

'Yea.'

'I'm Maura.'

'Hello Maura, if you don't mind I don't feel like dancing or talking.'

'Is that because Sandra said she didn't want to dance with you?'

'That's none of your business.'

'It might, she asked me to give you a message.'

'What message?'

'No, you're right, it's not my business.'

'What's the message?'

'I thought you didn't want to talk.'

Danny pulled a face.

'Ok, Sandra said she didn't want to dance with you because she can't dance. She wants to know if you'd teach her to dance or maybe have a mineral.'

Danny looked across at the other side of the hall and saw the girl in the blue dress looking anxiously in his direction.

'I would,' Danny blurted out.

'Would what?'

'Tell her I'd love to have a mineral and I'll teach her to dance anytime she'd like.'

Maura stood. 'Will you do me a favour?'

'Sure.'

'Ask your friend "Pencil Pants" if he'd like a mineral?'

'Do you mean Shay?'

'Shay, that's a cool name.'

'Right, see you in the mineral bar.'

'Yea you will, don't forget to bring Shay.'

Danny looked across the hall and the girl in the blue dress was still looking at him. He smiled. She smiled back at him. He jumped up on the bench and waved to her; she laughed and then she started to wave back at him.

CHAPTER 4

THE COAL SHED

Lily Rattigan's hand shook as she re-read the letter for the hundredth time. Four days ago when she saw the small square envelope drop into the hall she felt icy fear. When she read the letter, she came as close as she ever had to having a heart attack.

Lily,

It is time to put things right between us.
   I will be released from Mountjoy Prison on Monday the 6th of March. I plan to visit you at three that afternoon.
Dia duit,

Tadhg

She laid the letter on her living room table, looked out of the window and cursed the day Patrick built 'that bloody coal shed.' She glanced around the dowdy room of old furniture and faded wallpaper, when her eyes came to rest on the chipped statue of the Sacred Heart, she said a silent prayer.

Tadhg Mulligan was Lily Rattigan's late husband's best friend and the man she held responsible for his death.

━━╤╪╤━━

Patrick and Tadhg grew up together in nearby Cabra and from an early age, the two boys were inseparable. They did everything together; they played together, swam together, joined the scouts together and even ate in each other's homes. They had their differences too. Tadgh was calm and considered. Patrick was impulsive and unpredictable. Tadhg was a committed Republican and a Gaeilgeoir and Patrick was a Manchester United supporter who never set foot in Croke Park. Tadhg was bigger, almost a foot taller than Patrick and he always protected his more outspoken friend.

Lily was twenty years old when she first met Patrick. He and Tadhg were on a day trip to Howth when Lily and her friend sat in front of them on the open-topped, cream and blue Howth tram. Patrick was greatly taken by the petite Lily and she was taken by the red-haired Patrick. They quickly fell in love and within eighteen months they were married and renting Number Seven on the Avenue.

Tadhg, to no one's surprise, had been Patrick's best man.

On the day of their third wedding anniversary Lily was putting a broken chair into the newly built coal shed when she saw an unfamiliar pile of rags. She lifted the rags and underneath found two revolvers.

'Jesus, Mary and Joseph,' she gasped, staring at the guns.

'What is it?' Patrick asked, popping his head into the shed.

'Look at what I found.'

Patrick's face darkened and his brow furrowed.

'Christ, what are they doing there?'

'Are they yours?'

'No, of course not,' replied Patrick.

'Then how did they get there?'

'Go into the house. I'll put the guns under the loose floor-board in the back of the shed.'

A little later, Patrick followed Lily into the kitchen.

'Has Tadhg been here in the last few days?' he asked as he washed his hands in the sink.

'No. Tadhg wouldn't do this, not to us. Patrick this is serious. If the Gardaí find out we have guns in the house, we'll go to prison.'

'I know, let me think. First things first, I have to get a lock for the shed. Tadgh said he'd drop around some time this afternoon, if he does come keep him here until I get back.' Patrick grabbed his coat off the rack in the hall and left.

A still worried Lily was in the kitchen preparing their evening meal when Tadhg knocked on the front door. She opened the door and with a stern face and ordered him into the living room.

'I want you to get rid of those guns.'

'What are you talking about?' he asked, avoiding her eyes.

'You know what I'm talking about. You put them guns in the coal shed. I want them out of the house, right now.'

'Who told you they were mine?'

'Patrick told me.'

Beads of perspiration appeared on Tadhg's forehead. 'Lily, I can't keep guns in my house. The Gardaí know I have republican friends and they are constantly watching me. The guns are safer here.'

'I don't care; get them out of my house. Patrick put them under a loose board in the back of the shed. We have to visit his parents later today so I'll leave the key to the shed's new lock beside the clock on the mantelpiece. We'll be back by eight o'clock, see that the guns are gone before then'

'As soon it's dark I'll take them away.'

'You better leave now, Patrick will be back soon. All I need is for you two to get in a fight.'

When Lily and Patrick returned from visiting his parents the key on the mantelpiece had been moved. Lily breathed a little more easily.

The following day Lily and Patrick were eating their evening meal when three members of An Garda Síochána broke open the front door of their home. The much-hated overweight Sergeant Mooney strutted into the house and ordered Patrick to remain at the table.

'Where are the guns?' Mooney asked, leaning on the table.

'I don't know what you're talking about,' snapped Patrick.

'We can do this the easy way or the hard way. Which is it to be? It's up to you. For the last time, where are the guns?'

'I just told you I don't know anything about guns.'

Sergeant Mooney slid his truncheon from his belt and pounded it into Patrick's shoulder.

Patrick groaned and grimaced in pain.

Mooney nodded to the other two Gardaí. One of them stormed up the stairs, the other guard ransacked the living room and parlour. Five minutes later one of the guards smashed open the new lock on the shed. He strolled into the shed and when he noticed the new nails in the old wood he took a crowbar and lifted the floorboard. When the guard entered the living room with the guns Patrick was shaken to the core.

'I'm telling you, Mooney, they're nothing to do with...'

'Tried to make a fool of me, did yea?' Sergeant Mooney swung his truncheon and hit Patrick on the head twice. Lilly screamed. Patrick fell to the floor.

Unconscious and bleeding he was taken to the Mater Hospital. The following day after suffering a massive brain haemorrhage Patrick died. Overwhelmed with grief and rage, Lily stormed into Mountjoy Station and demanded to speak to Sgt Mooney. When the sergeant came to the desk she told him the guns belonged to Tadhg Mulligan.

Tadhg went to ground but three days later when he attended the funeral of his friend he was arrested. During his two-day trial, Tadhg pleaded guilty but refused to answer any questions. Lily was not called as a witness. When she learned that Tadhg had been sentenced to eight years in prison, she wept.

After Patrick's death and Tadhg's trial, Lily went from being an out-going, joyous woman to being a nervous person who was afraid of everyone. Her life was filled with guilt and shame and she spent her days looking over her shoulder. The people of the Avenue changed towards her; some thought her unfortunate but others thought of her as an informer and muttered 'stool pigeon' or 'grasser' as she passed. Others deliberately ignored her and still more called her a traitor. Her life was solitary, she never had any visitors and her home was always silent. Even when she was kneeling in church praying to her God she felt eyes scrutinizing her and condemning her.

On Thursday the 9th March 1950 at five past three, Tadhg Mulligan stood at the top of the Avenue. To him the place looked as it always did – dull, sweet and beautiful; little had changed, the houses looked the same, the children playing in the street looked exactly like the children he remembered and even Mr Farrell's bicycle outside his house looked as it had always done. He stood a moment and breathed in the Avenue's ordinariness. Then, with downcast eyes and shoulders sagging, he moved down the Avenue. When he reached Number Seven he removed his hand from his pocket, lifted the heavy knocker and let it fall on its brass base. The knock thundered through the house.

Lily stood and as she passed the little wooden crucifix hanging on the wall she touched the feet of the crucified Christ. Pale and tired she pulled open the front door.

'Are you going to let me in?' Tadhg said as he lifted his eyes to her.

'I am,' she replied and took a step back.

Tadhg removed his cap and stepped into the hallway. 'You haven't changed a thing in the house,' he said, as he entered the living room. 'It looks exactly as I remember it.'

'Why would I change things? It's how Patrick liked it.' Lily sat in the armchair by the dark fireplace and placed her hands on her knees. 'You should not have come.'

'Is it alright if I sit?'

Lily nodded slightly. Tadhg removed his coat and draped it over a chair and sat.

'You wanted to talk, so talk,' Lily said after a while.

'I have things to say that might offend.'

'I can't afford the luxury of being offended. Say your piece and leave.'

'I'll get right to the point. The guns you found in your coal shed were Patrick's guns, not mine. He asked me to get them for him.'

Shocked Lily's eyes darted to Tadhg's face.

'I don't believe you. What in God's name would Patrick want with guns?'

'I don't know.' Tadhg looked away, 'Patrick knew about us.'

Bile gathered in Lily's throat. 'How do you know that?'

'He told me.' Tadhg pulled a handkerchief out of his pocket and rubbed his forehead. 'He said if I'd leave the country and never return he'd say nothing to you. He also demanded I get him two revolvers. I told him how dangerous it was to have possession of guns but he insisted. So, I did as he asked and when the guns arrived two days earlier than expected I told Patrick I had them. I explained to him I couldn't keep them in my house and he said I had to wait until he'd found a place to hide them. I couldn't wait and when he didn't get back to me, on Sunday morning when you were at Mass, I let myself in and put the guns in your coal shed.'

'Why didn't you came back and remove the guns?'

'I came back as you asked, found the key to the shed on the mantelpiece but I couldn't find any loose floorboards in the shed. I thought Patrick moved the guns to a safer place so I put the key back and left.'

Lily shivered. 'Why didn't you tell me you didn't find the guns?'

'I tried but when I got here the guards were already searching the house.' Tadhg fell silent a moment. 'During the trail, I learned it was Patrick who informed on me.'

Lily's heart turned over. 'No, that's wrong. I was the one who went to Sgt Mooney and told him the guns were yours.'

'I know, but the day I told Patrick the guns arrived he went to the Garda station and reported me to the desk-sergeant.'

'Why would he do that?'

'To punish me; to punish us. He told the Gardaí the guns were in my house but when they raided my home and found nothing they raided the homes of my comrades and friends. That's why they raided this house. Lily, I would have done anything for you. I looked for the guns but couldn't find them. I didn't know what to do and I didn't want another fight with Patrick.'

'Then why did you plead guilty?'

'What good would it have done to do otherwise? Patrick was dead. I knew I was going to prison. If the Gardaí knew Patrick was involved you would have been deprived of your widow's pension.'

'What are you talking about?'

'Widows' pensions are not paid to wives of subversives. I came here today to tell you the truth and to let you know the guns were never mine.'

'Patrick was a good man,' Lily said unable to look at Tadhg. 'He couldn't have done that to you.'

'Patrick was a good man but he was also a man I deceived and hurt. I'm deeply sorry for everything that happened. I never meant to hurt you or Patrick.' Tadhg stood up. 'I've said my piece, I'll be off.'

Lily reached out and touched his burly hand.

'Stay a little, we'll light a fire?'

Lily went out to the coal shed, brought in some kindling wood and a few sods of dry turf. Tadhg set the fire and lit it. Then the two old friends sat in silence; they listened to the crackling of the fire and mourned their loss and the missing years.

CHAPTER 5

MR DUNNOCK'S DAY

'Did you ever hear the likes? He asked me if we stocked Chablis,' snapped Mrs Moore a few seconds after Mr Dunnock had stepped out of their grocery shop. 'And when I asked him what Chablis is, he said in that uppity voice of his, "It's wine, fine wine, Madam". I told him, the only alcohol we sell is stout and sherry and he said to me, if you don't improve your selection of wines I will be forced to take my custom elsewhere.' Mrs Moore's face glowed with frustration. 'Who in God's name does that man think he is? All he has ever bought here are cream crackers and a few slices of cheese. And now, declare to God, he wants a "selection of wines"! I ask you! What kind of an eejit is he? And what kind of a name is Dunnock, anyway?'

Mr Moore did not respond to his wife's observations or questions; he simply smiled and went in search of his sweeping brush.

───✠✠───

The tall, serious Mr Dunnock was in his mid-fifties and lived in Number Two. He was a methodical man and a creature of habit. He rose every morning at seven o'clock sharp, washed, shaved and ate his breakfast. At twenty five past eight, he donned his coat, positioned his wide-brimmed bowler on his head and set off for work. At nine on the dot, he pulled apart the small curtains of his cashier's hatch in the offices of the Dublin Gas Company and began his day's work, taking money from customers and stamping their bills as paid. When the clock struck five, Mr Dunnock counted his cash, totalled his day's ledger and, at exactly half past five, exited his workplace and walked home. After hanging his coat on the rack in the hall he walked into the living room, sat at the table and listened to the slow *tick, tick, tick* of his late mother's mantel clock. Some evenings after his meal, Mr Dunnock selected a book from the bookcase in the parlour, sat by the fire and read and on other evenings he listened to the radio. But every evening he was in bed by ten o'clock and as he drifted towards sleep he tried not to think about Moiré. Mr Dunnock lived a life most people would consider boring, but to him his life was calm and predictable and, while there was little joy or excitement in it, it was safe and he was determined to keep it that way.

━╬ ╬━

Most of Mr Dunnock's colleagues considered him eccentric, but Miss Brent felt differently. Every morning Miss Brent opened her hatch at five to nine and waited for Mr Dunnock to open his hatch at nine on the dot and when he did, her heart gave a little flutter.

Miss Brent was an unmarried woman in her late forties, originally from Limerick. Every morning and afternoon she made the tea for the staff breaks and always handed Mr Dunnock his cup of milky tea with two sugars; then she sat and listened to him and the assistant manager Mr Frank West discuss the issues of the day.

━╬ ╬━

On the morning of the 3rd January, 1950 the smile of a young woman shattered Mr Dunnock's carefully constructed internal peace. He had been removing his break-time package of cheese and crackers from his briefcase when she slid an envelope under the brass grill fixed between him and the customers.

'Good morning,' she said, as she removed her scarf and shook out her hair. She was an attractive, brown-haired young woman with eyes that sparkled with life.

An image of Moiré flashed into Mr Dunnock's mind. *Moiré standing alone on Dollymount strand.* His shook his head, the package of crackers slipped through his fingers, sailed downward and bounced off the toe of his highly-polished shoe. A second image flashed into his mind. *Moiré sobbing as the wind blew her hair wildly.*

'Is something the matter?' inquired the young woman.

'No, nothing is the matter,' he said. 'What can I do for you?'

'I'd like to pay my bill. I hope you don't mind me saying this but you look like you've just seen a ghost.'

'I don't believe in ghosts and it's none of your business how I look.'

She winced. 'Sorry, I didn't mean to intrude.'

Mr Dunnock held onto the counter and tried to dismiss the third image of Moiré that had just exploded in his mind. *Moiré pulling the engagement ring off her finger and holding it out to him.* Breathing uneasily, he let go of the counter, stamped the young woman's bill and returned it.

Mr Dunnock then did something that caused Miss Brent at hatch number 3 to drop her fountain pen; he spoke apologetically to a customer.

'Sorry if I was abrupt. You were right. I am feeling a little unwell. Please forgive me if I was rude.'

'I'm sorry you're not feeling well,' the young woman said with a smile.

Mr Dunnock stood behind the brass grill of his hatch and, like a lonely prisoner peering out through the bars of his prison cell, watched the pretty young woman walk out of the building and disappear into the bustling crowd on the street. He closed the small curtains, picked the package of crackers off the floor and went to the staff room. He was sitting quietly thinking about the empty hollow at the centre of his life when Miss Brent opened the door and came into the room.

'Did that young woman say something to upset you?' she asked in her sing-song Limerick accent.

'No, not at all,' said Mr Dunnock softly.

'Would you care for a cup of tea?'

Mr Dunnock shook his head. Miss Brent removed the kettle from the cupboard and filled it with water, all the time talking incessantly about the weather, the state of the roads and tea making.

'I know it's a bit early but I'm having a cup. Would you care for one, Mr Dunnock? My late mother use to say a nice cup of tea lifts the spirit.'

'You talk an awful lot, Miss Brent,' snapped Mr Dunnock.

'Do I? Well, you're early for your break and I don't like people watching me while I make the tea. It makes me nervous, so I talk.'

'Miss Brent, we've known each other for twenty years, why on earth would you be nervous of me?'

'We do not know each other.' Her voice was trembling. 'You don't even know my first name! We have never had a proper conversation. Good morning and good afternoon is all we ever say to each other.'

'I've no idea what you're talking about and I've had enough of this inane chitchat.'

Mr Dunnock returned to the shop floor and standing at his hatch he thought what a ridiculous man he had become.

At fifteen minutes past one, Mr Dunnock arrived at his usual bench in Stephen's Green to eat his lunch only to see Miss Brent on his bench eating a sandwich. He was about to walk away when a large seagull swooped and snatched the sandwich from Miss Brent's hand. She shrieked and Mr Dunnock rushed to her side.

'Are you alright, Miss Brent?'

'I'm perfectly alright, Mr Dunnock,' she said stiffly, brushing crumbs off her coat.

He remained standing in front of her.

Slowly, she raised her eyes. 'Did you want something, Mr Dunnock?'

'No. Yes. I want to apologise for being rude this morning. I am sorry.'

'Apology accepted.'

He continued to stand there.

'What is the matter with you, Mr Dunnock, are you ill?'

'No, I'm not ill,' he said. 'May I join you?'

Raising her eyebrows, Miss Brent moved along the bench to make room. Mr Dunnock sat beside her. She looked straight ahead.

'Have you ever been in love?' he asked.

Miss Brent moved several inches further away from Mr Dunnock. 'What a thing to ask anyone.'

'I'm not asking anyone, I'm asking you.'

'Why would you pose such a personal question?' She folded her arms tightly, the closeness of his body made her feel a little giddy.

'Because I'd like to know the answer.'

'I'm not prepared to answer that question.'

'Twenty five years ago I loved a woman. Her name was Moiré, she was lovely but I was dreadful to her. I always thought, hoped, one day we would meet again but we never did. Not a single day goes by that I don't think about her, even though I try very hard not to do so.'

'I don't know what to say,' said Miss Brent.

'You don't have to say anything. I'll leave you now.' Mr Dunnock stood. 'Would you care for my sandwich?'

'Yes, I would,' said Miss Brent; she added very softly, 'But only if you'll stay and share it with me?'

Mr Dunnock cleared his throat nervously.

Miss Brent unfolded her hands and placed her hands on her lap, waiting.

'I'd like that, Maureen,' he said finally; he opened his briefcase and placed his carefully-wrapped sandwich on the bench between them.

Miss Brent took a deep breath. 'Freddy, the answer to your question is yes. I have loved and I have lost.'

Miss Brent and Mr Dunnock sat, shared the sandwich and watched two mallard ducks glide effortlessly on the still waters of the artificial lake.

CHAPTER 6

ODD RELATIVES AND WOOLLY TOGS

Eight-year-old Brendan Clooney, who lived in the house with the bright red door, thought his mother was very odd. For one thing, she was always knitting. Day and night she knit. A strange thing about his mother's knitted garments was they never felt new, and they never felt new because they were made out of recycled wool. Yesterday's pullover was tomorrow's socks and yesterday's scarf was tomorrow's gloves. He and his younger siblings Donal and Deirdre were always wearing the same wool, only they were wearing it on different parts of their bodies.

Another thing Brendan thought odd about his mother was that she was a snob; she didn't mix with the neighbours.

'They are common, they don't take summer holidays,' his mother would say as he stood with his skinny arms outstretched while she wound a ball of wool from the skein draped over his wrists.

Most of their neighbours never took holidays but the Clooneys always did. Every year in July with their suitcases secured with an assortment of frayed belts and old ties the family travelled on the long-distance, single-decker, rear-loading, bottle-green CIE bus to Bray, County Wicklow. For three young Dublin children, Bray was an exciting if not an exotic place and best of all they could swim every day for two weeks!

One of Mrs Clooney's oddest knitting ideas was knitted swimwear, or as the children called them 'woolly togs'. Apart from the fact woolly togs made them itchy in places they couldn't scratch in public, the swimwear had a basic design flaw. When wool gets wet it gets heavy. Consequently every time the children leapt into the water the knitted togs shot to their feet or worse, ended up on the sea bed. Donal and Deirdre were too young to care, but Brendan regarded the times he spent searching for his swimwear along the Bray coastline to be among the most embarrassing moments of his childhood. Worse, his mother refused to believe he wasn't losing his togs on purpose, and he got a smack on the head every time he complained.

⇒⇍⇏⇐

Brendan's mother had an unmarried sister, Ann, who was also very odd. Aunt Ann's main peculiarity was that she often misused words or even made them up.

One spring day as Brendan was washing the parlour windows of the Clooney home, Aunt Ann strolled by and said, 'That water is dirty, you should reblemish it.'

On another day when Brendan was playing with his lead soldiers in the back garden, he overheard Aunt Ann and his mother talking.

'Is he a good doctor?' Brendan's mother asked as she sat on the window ledge of the house and lit up a Woodbine cigarette.

'Oh he's excellent, he's the very pineapple of his procession,' replied Aunt Ann.

Aunt Ann was, as she put it, 'musically elevacated' and a professionally trained singer. In truth, she had one good note at the bottom of her voice and one good note at the top of her voice and all the intervening notes were of dubious quality. She also had a problem singing in key. But Aunt Ann was confident she was a wonderful singer.

Every second Friday night Brendan, Donal and Deirdre were marched into the parlour, seated on the settee and subjected to what Aunt Ann referred to as 'a musical recycle'. During the first part of the 'recycle' his mother would sit at the out-of-tune piano and Aunt Ann would stand in front of the piano and sing great 'areas' from the operas. For the second part of the 'recycle', Aunt Ann produced her violin and the two sisters gallantly murdered many traditional Irish airs; the children found these evenings excruciating.

'Ann's voice is better than it sounds,' Uncle Michael use to say, whenever he had to listen to his sister sing.

Uncle Michael too was an odd person; he was a plumber who thought he was a great artist. His home was filled with huge unfinished oil paintings of imagined places and creatures. Even though Uncle Michael never exhibited or sold a painting in his life, he was extremely proud of his artworks. On one of the Clooney family's annual visits to Uncle Michael's home, Brendan asked the great man why his paintings were never finished. His uncle took a moment, considered the question and then answered.

'Good question, you see Patrick when...'

'My name is Brendan.'

'I always thought your name was Patrick.'

'No. Brendan is my name.'

'Why haven't you corrected me when I called you Patrick in the past?'

'You have never called me Patrick in the past.'

By this time Uncle Michael had forgotten what they were talking about and so Brendan never got an answer to his question.

━┼┝━

In 1950, midway through the Clooneys' annual holiday, they had their usual two-day visit from Aunt Ann. The children did not enjoy Aunt Ann's visits, she would monopolised their mother's time. With a great flourish she he would give each child a few pennies and said, 'Go off and rejoin yourselves.'

The funniest part of Aunt Ann's holiday visits was always her insistence on joining the children for their daily swim. Her changing into a swimming costume under a towel on Bray's stony beach was an exercise in modesty and contortionism.

'Don't be looking at me, you make me nervous,' she would bark as the children stood giggling and laughing at their twisting, coiling aunt. The twisting and coiling was followed by endless swimsuit adjustments, never-ending bathing cap repositioning and finally a mortifying walk to the water. Aunt Ann's first contact with the water produced a cacophony of yelps and screams that made Brendan's embarrassment at wearing knitted togs evaporate instantly.

On the second day of Aunt Ann's visit, Brendan's mother opened her beach bag and brought out a beautiful, bright-yellow, hand-knitted swimsuit.

'It's for you Ann, it's made of virgin wool,' Brendan's mother said as she proudly laid the swimsuit out on the beach stones. Aunt Ann expressed herself ecstatic.

'It's gorgeous Agnes, it looks like a resigner outfit.'

'Why don't we go for a swim right now?' suggested little Deirdre, keen to see what was going to happen to Ann in her woolly togs. 'It's great fun if you dive straight in, Aunt Ann. Don't go carefully, just jump.'

'I'm sure it is,' Aunt Ann answered calmly. 'You children go along and have your swim. I'll join you in a minute.'

'Agnes, if I wore that swimming costume I'd be the biggest exhibitionist on the beach.' Ann said the instant the children were out of earshot.

'What do you mean?'

'It wouldn't stay on me very long, would it?'

Agnes sat up straight and stared at her sister.

'You mean the children aren't doing it to annoy me?'

'No Agnes, they aren't.'

'Not even Brendan?'

'No, Agnes.'

Agnes Clooney leapt to her feet, called the children out of the water and, once they had dried and dressed, marched them to the nearest drapery shop where she bought each child their first store-bought swimming togs. Brendan was overjoyed and out of gratitude to dear Aunt Ann the next time she and their mother gave a musical 'recycle' he stood and applauded until his hands were sore.

CHAPTER 7
CAITRÍONA'S SECRET

Caitríona Spillane and her nine-year-old daughter Bronagh lived at Number Fifteen, the house with the emerald green door. She was a kind, polite, happy person who had a smile and time for everyone. Whenever anyone was sick, she was the first to arrive and offer help. She went to the chemist shop for Mrs Richards and to the Medical Supply Company in Talbot Street for Mrs Green.

Father Kevin was a curate in the nearby parish of the Church of the Most Precious Blood, in Cabra West. He was a handsome if somewhat moody, unpredictable man. Every Wednesday Bronagh eagerly awaited the arrival of her uncle Father Kevin. The priest enjoyed the time he spent with Bronagh and took great delight in watching her grow up. In wintertime he took her to museums, the cinema or sometimes to a cine-variety show in the Theatre Royal. In the summertime he took her to the zoo, the botanical gardens or the seaside.

Bronagh loved her uncle and the special times they spent together.

Of late, Caitríona noticed that Kevin seemed preoccupied and out of sorts. One evening after Bronagh went to bed Caitríona spoke to him about her concerns.

'I don't mean to pry but what is wrong with you, Kevin?' Caitríona asked as she sat opposite him.

'Nothing is wrong with me,' he replied, leaning back in his chair.

'Well, it doesn't seem like nothing. You've hardly said a word since you arrived. Has something happened?'

'Yes, Father Duffy, my Parish Priest, didn't recommend me for advancement and when I asked why he said he was unhappy with me and my work.'

'Unhappy with your work, what does he mean?'

'He said my sermons were lazy and I'm far too short with people. He also said he doesn't like me to stay here overnight, away from the parish. He maintains I should be available at all times to parishioners. He wants me to live exclusively in the parish house.'

When Father Kevin left, Caitríona busied herself about the place. Her mind was in a whirl. She didn't know what she would do if Kevin stopped visiting.

Caitríona was in the back garden digging up a few potatoes for the evening meal when she heard the knock on the front door. Thinking her brother was early, and had as usual misplaced his latch key, Caitríona swung the door open and was confronted by a neatly dressed man about her own age.

'Hello Caitríona,' the man said breezily.

Caitríona was lost for words. Darragh Molloy, the boy who on her tenth birthday had asked her to marry him, was standing on her doorstep. 'I told Mrs O'Neill I'd drop these things off to you,' he said.

Caitríona stared speechlessly at her visitor.

He added helpfully, 'They belonged to your Uncle Vincent. Mrs O'Neill in Athlone said she wrote to you and told you I'd be bringing them along.'

Caitríona pulled herself together and smiled apologetically. 'Yes, she did write, I just wasn't expecting you so soon. Where are my manners?' She opened the door fully. 'It's nice of you to go to all this trouble, Darragh. All the way from Athlone to here.'

'It's no trouble, it's a pleasure.' He dropped an awkward kiss on her cheek as he stepped into the house. 'I'm off to Holyhead on the nine o'clock sailing tonight and delivering this box gave me an excuse to call on you. You look nice, really lovely.'

Caitríona pushed some stray hairs off her face as she opened the parlour door. 'You can put the box in here. Why are you going to Wales?'

He set the box on the small coffee table. 'I'm in the British Navy and I'm on my way back to my base in Holyhead.' He straightened up, looking toward the three framed photos on the mantelpiece over the tiled fireplace. 'Is that man your husband?'

'Yes, that's Richard. He passed away.'

'I heard. I'm sorry. It must have been difficult for you.'

'It was.'

'He looks like a nice fellow. I was surprised when you married him. I always thought you'd marry Eugene.'

Caitríona did not reply. She'd thought so too, a long time ago.

Everyone in Athlone had said Caitríona and Darragh were made for each other, that is until Eugene Carr arrived in the town. Eugene was a charming, good-looking young man with the deepest brown eyes Caitríona had ever seen. He excelled in all things GAA and from the first moment Caitríona laid eyes on the rugged young sportsman she was besotted. It all began when Eugene scored the winning goal during the Saturday football game. As the spectators cheered, Eugene caught Caitríona's eye. She smiled at him and he smiled back at her. That night in the GAA hall he asked her to dance and she accepted. She danced twice more with him and when Darragh asked her why she danced so much with the stranger she answered, 'I was only being friendly.'

Caitríona continued being friendly with Eugene and one night when she and Darragh were out walking along the river's edge she told him she had kissed Eugene. Two weeks later she told Darragh she was not sure she wanted to keep seeing him exclusively.

'What exactly do you mean, not seeing me exclusively?'

'I don't know, I think I want to see other people,' replied Caitríona.

She and Darragh remained friends for a while. They did all the things they had always done before: they went to the cinema, met their friends for drinks and a chat and often went for walks but things had changed between them. One warm evening, as they strolled along the banks of the Shannon, Darragh spoke up.

'I don't like this new arrangement. I don't know if I'm coming or going. You have to make up your mind. I am either your boyfriend or I'm not.'

'If I have to choose then you're not my boyfriend,' Caitríona replied and left a devastated Darragh standing at the river's edge.

During the next few months, they often found themselves in each other's company. Caitríona was always pleasant and polite but it was clear to Darragh that she had lost all interest in him.

Meanwhile, Caitríona was having problems with Eugene. He was not an easy boyfriend; he had unexpected shifting moods. One day he could be pleasant and joyous and the next day he could be argumentative and condescending.

One night when Darragh and a few friends were in Sean's Pub in town a drunken Eugene started to make fun of Caitríona. He mocked the way she spoke and made snide remarks about her family. Then when she didn't laugh at his jokes he grabbed her by the arms and shouted, 'Why are you here if you don't like my jokes? Why don't you go home and give me a bit of peace?'

'Don't speak to Caitríona like that,' Darragh said and grabbed Eugene by the tie, pulling him forward. 'Apologise right now.'

'Well if it isn't Caitríona's old lapdog? You'd love to take Caitríona home, wouldn't you? You might even get a little kiss.'

'You're a waste of space,' Darragh said and ploughed his fist into Eugene's face. Eugene fell backwards, collided with a table and crashed to the floor. Caitríona raced to Eugene's side and glared at Darragh.

The following Saturday as Caitríona was preparing to go out for the evening, her sister Patricia burst into her bedroom.

'What's the matter? You look as miserable as a frost-bitten apple,' said Caitríona.

'Lizzie Fleming told me Eugene was taking her to the dance in the GAA tonight,' Patricia said, afraid to look at Caitríona.

'Why would you believe Lizzie Fleming? She's the biggest liar in town.' Looking confident, Caitríona resumed combing her hair.

'I believed Lizzie because Eugene was sitting beside her when she said it.'

That evening, a furious Caitríona marched into the GAA hall. Darragh intercepted her at the cloakroom and guided her to a seat on the right side of the hall. 'Patricia told me what happened. Don't do anything in anger.'

Yet while Darragh was trying to talk her down, Caitríona's eyes hunted for Eugene and Lizzie. Then she saw them. He was sitting in an alcove near the back of the hall and Lizzie was sitting beside him. However Eugene was not looking at Lizzie he was staring at Caitríona. She flashed her eyes at him. He grinned, turned and kissed Lizzie on the lips. Caitríona coupled her hands around Darragh's neck, pulled him forward and kissed him. She then took his hand and they danced together.

Eugene's eyes followed Caitríona all night.

Walking home from the dance Darragh stopped by the water's edge and said, 'I know when you kissed me you didn't mean it.'

Caitríona dropped her gaze.

'You know you're playing with fire and nobody can control fire.'

'I know,' she confessed humbly.

A few days later Darragh was walking along the river bank when he saw Caitríona on the opposite side. He was about to wave when Eugene appeared, took her in his arms and kissed her. She kissed him back. Standing alone, Darragh realised Caitríona was never going to be his; Eugene was always going to be there.

That autumn, Darragh went to London and within a year had joined the British Navy. His mother kept him informed on what was going on in Athlone. At Christmas, she told him Caitríona and Eugene had broken up and she had moved to Dublin. While he was stationed in Gibraltar he got word Caitríona had married and two years later he learned her husband had been killed in a work accident.

⚓

Darragh studied the framed photos on the mantelpiece. 'Is the little girl your daughter?'

'Yes, that's Bronagh. She's bigger now.'

'She looks like you.'

'That's what people say.'

'I didn't know you had a child. I'm surprised my mother didn't tell me.'

Caitríona shrugged. Darragh picked up the photo of Caitríona, Bronagh and a priest.

'How is your family?' Caitríona asked before he could ask another question.

He turned to her. 'Oh, both my parents died within a few years of each other. I have a distant aunt still living in Athlone. I visit her every year or so. She and Mrs O'Neill are great friends.'

'I meant a family of your own?'

'I never married. The Navy is my family. I enjoy the life.'

'Do you have time for a cup of tea?'

Darragh glanced at his watch. 'Yes, a quick cup.'

'I'll put the kettle on.'

The sound of the front door opening brought her back into the room from the kitchen, and out into the hallway.

'You ran all the way home, didn't you?' she smiled, as she hung her daughter's coat on the rack.

'Is Uncle Kevin here?' asked a red-faced Bronagh as she bounced past her mother into the living room. She stopped abruptly when she saw Darragh.

Caitríona came in behind her. 'No, I told you this morning he won't be here till seven, but this is someone I'd like you to meet. He's an old friend of mine from Athlone. Bronagh say hello to Darragh Molloy.'

Bronagh stood looking up at Darragh and he thought he was looking at the young Caitríona he had fallen in love with all those years ago. The resemblance between mother and daughter was uncanny. She had Caitríona's face, hair, lips; even the way she cocked her head was pure Caitríona.

'Hello, Mr Molloy,' Bronagh smiled and lowering her voice added, 'Are you one of Mother's old boyfriends?'

'Bronagh, that's a cheeky question to ask,' Caitríona gently chided her daughter.

'I'll answer the question. Your mother and I were best friends, we grew up together in Athlone but that was all so long ago. It's very nice to meet you, Bronagh. How old are you?'

'I'm nine years old. How old are you?' asked Bronagh.

'Bronagh you don't ask adults their age,' Caitríona said, smiling apologetically at Darragh.

'That's alright, Bronagh, I'm two years older than your mother.'

'Then you're forty one, Mr Molloy.'

'Correct again and call me Darragh. Mr Molloy was my father.'

'That's enough questions for now, Bronagh,' interjected Caitríona.

'Are you going to take my mother out on a date?'

'Bronagh stop, now you're being rude. Mr Molloy stopped by to drop off a package. He's on his way back to Holyhead.'

'That's a pity,' said Bronagh. 'No one ever takes Mother out.'

'Go, change out of your school uniform and if you promise to be polite I'll let you join us for a cup of tea,' Caitríona said, pretending to be annoyed.

'OK but don't talk about me when I'm not here,' Bronagh said as she rushed up the stairs.

'She's beautiful, she looks like you,' Darragh said as he sat at the table.

'She's a bit of a handful.'

'A bit like someone I once knew.'

Caitríona flicked her eyes at Darragh and returned to the kitchen to finish making the tea.

'What time will Uncle Kevin be here?' Bronagh asked as she bounded back down the stairs.

'I told you, he said he'd be here about seven. So you have a good two hours to do your homework,' called Caitríona from the kitchen.

'Who's Uncle Kevin?' asked Darragh.

'Uncle Kevin is Mammy's brother. He's a priest. Don't you know Uncle Kevin?'

'No, but I left Athlone a long time ago.'

'Does Darragh know Uncle Kevin?' Bronagh asked Caitríona, as she returned with the teapot and cups on a tray.

Caitríona looked away as she set the tray down.

Darragh studied Bronagh's strikingly beautiful brown eyes. He remembered the photos in the parlour of the child and the priest and he suddenly understood everything. He glanced at the clock on the mantelpiece.

'Is it really that late? Oh, I can't stay for tea. I have to be off.'

'Do you really have to go?' asked Bronagh.

'Yes, I forgot. I have another stop to make.'

In the narrow hall, he removed his coat from the stand.

'Thanks for bringing the box of things,' said Caitríona, standing beside him.

'Think nothing of it. It was nice seeing you and meeting Bronagh.'

The front opened and a man dressed in a black suit stepped into the hall, and did a double take.

'Darragh, now there's a face from the past, I can't say it's nice to see you again. What are you doing here?'

'Hello, Eugene.'

'Why did Darragh call Father Kevin, "Eugene"?' Bronagh piped up, tugging at her grey-faced mother's sleeve.

'Because Kevin is the name I took when I became a priest. It's my priest name,' Eugene said as he hung his coat on the stand.

Darragh glanced at Caitríona, then at Bronagh and then at Eugene. Eugene smirked and brushed past him into the living room. 'Bronagh, come, I have something to show you,' he called over his shoulder.

Bronagh skipped after him into the living room and Darragh was left alone with Caitríona. He stared at her, holding his feelings in check. 'She doesn't know, does she?'

'No.'

'You never did stop playing with fire, did you? Goodbye Caitríona,' he said and quietly closed the door behind him.

CHAPTER 8

THE BOX OF CHOCOLATES

I was putting on my coat to visit the neighbours, Frank and Bridget. It was Bridget's unmarried sister's birthday and they were celebrating. While waiting patiently for my good wife, I happened to glance into her bag and saw the box of chocolates. *Oh heavens,* I said to myself, *what should I do?*

'Darling,' I said to my ever-busy spouse, 'do you think it's a good idea to give such an expensive box of chocolates to Maureen? She's already rather … em … overweight. She might be mortified.'

'Think of it like this Archie. I'm saving your waistline at the expense of hers,' my wife said as she gently patted my tummy.

'My waistline does not need saving.'

'Yes it does, Archie. You're under doctor's orders. Now, are you ready to go?'

'Yes I'm ready and I have been ready for five minutes. I have been waiting for you.'

'Then it's a wonder you didn't think of locking the back door or checking the windows. Men have it so easy.'

'Not if he's married to you, he doesn't,' I muttered.

'I heard that. Are you not wearing a hat?'

'Rachael, we are going across the Avenue to a neighbour's house, we are not journeying to Outer Mongolia.'

'Sometimes Archie, the things you say are beyond ridiculous. Come on or we'll be the last to arrive.'

———✥✥———

We were late, and everyone else was already in the parlour, chatting and imbibing. Frank, our host handed me a glass of whiskey and Rachael gave Bridget's sister Maureen the beautiful box of Fuller's Cream Sugars and Chocolates.

'Oh, I love Fuller's sweets,' the birthday girl said before disappearing into the kitchen.

The room was warm, the company was convivial and the food was delightful. Everything was going quite beautifully, when a screech came from the kitchen. I braced myself. They must have opened the box of chocolates. Within seconds the slightly overweight Bridget and her even more overweight sister Maureen rushed into the living room with such haste that the two women got stuck in the doorway.

After she'd freed herself, Maureen took up a position in front of me; she was holding the box of chocolates in her hands.

'Rachael I'm sure you were unaware of this and I hold Archie completely responsible for it.' Ceremoniously, she opened the box of chocolates and revealed an almost empty tray with a solitary chocolate sitting in the right hand corner.

'Archie? What have you done?' asked my wife in a voice so sharp it could cut leather.

'There is a perfectly good explanation,' I said, trying to appear calm while wondering how on earth I was going to vindicate myself.'

'Well, what is it?' demanded the birthday girl.

'What's wrong with the chocolates?' asked another neighbour, Brenda, rummaging in her handbag. 'Let me get my glasses.'

'Archie's been up to something,' answered Brenda's ever-patient husband. 'And stop rummaging in your bag, there's nothing to see.'

'What do you mean there's nothing to see? What is everybody talking about?'

'If you'll all give me a minute, I'll explain,' I said.

'Let's see how he gets out of this,' Frank, our host said grinning like a Cheshire cat.

'I found them,' exclaimed Brenda as she put on her glasses. 'But I still don't know what's going on.'

'Be patient, everyone. This will take a moment or two,' I said, knowing full well it would take a lot more than that. 'Last week, while my good wife was at her weekly whist drive, I was sitting by the fire listening to Peadar O'Connor's *Making and Mending* programme on Raidió Eireann. Peadar helps people fix things around the house or on a farm and starts every reply with "first you get an oily rag". While Peadar was explaining how to change the plugs on a Massy Ferguson tractor, my mind wandered. I remembered my wife had recently been gifted a small but beautiful box of Fuller's Cream Sugars and Milk Chocolates. I wondered *whatever happened to the chocolates?* Then I recalled that my good wife had mentioned she had put them somewhere to keep them safe. "Keep them safe" in Rachael's world is a euphemism for keeping them from me. I wondered where the beautiful Rachael might hide the chocolates. She is good at hiding things, so good that most of my searches have resulted in total failure. Undeterred I set about my search. I looked in cupboards, cabinets, closets, cubbyholes, drawers, wardrobes and the sideboard, all without success. I looked in the kitchen, the living room, the parlour, even the bedrooms and then...I remembered the place underneath the stairs where the gas meter resides. I opened the small door and there, on a tiny shelf, was the box of Cream Sugars and Milk Chocolates. Success! Delighted with my detecting skills, I returned to my seat by the fire.

'With the box of Fuller's Chocolates on my lap, I first examined the elegant case. On the front was a colourful ribbon and photograph of the delightful contents. On the rear was an inventory detailing each delight; sugar-dusted Orange Creams, milk chocolate-covered Sea-Salt Caramels, Irish Strawberry Sugar Creams and Brazilian Dark Chocolate-covered Fudge. I lifted the box to my nose and inhaled the glorious aroma. Placing it again on my knees I noticed that the ribbon was only attached to the top of the box and as the lid was not hermetically sealed, I could open it. *Could I risk a peep?* I wondered. And answered myself, *yes!*

'I carefully removed the top of the box and there was the treasure of the night. In three rows of the four, sat the magnificent sugars and the incredible chocolates, all demanding to be consumed. My eyes glided across the tray and I identified each little pleasure. I admired the Strawberry Sugar and the Sea-Salt Caramel chocolates and before I realised it, the Strawberry Sugar was melting in my mouth. Initially, it was sweet then the sharp fruity strawberry cream was oh so smooth.'

I was interrupted at this point by a gasp of pain and outrage from Maureen, but I hardened my heart and carried quickly on.

'This was followed by the most delightful Sea-Salt Caramel. As the chocolate melted in my mouth it released the most delicate flavour. Yet as the caramel trickled down my throat, guilt gripped my heart. I quickly but carefully slipped the top back on the box and returned it and its remaining contents to its hiding place.'

'Two nights later, sitting at the fireside while my good wife was at her sodality meeting, I was again listening to the radio. This time it was Din Joe and his dancing on the radio programme, *Take the Floor.* Not being interested in Din Joe or his programme and feeling a little neglected and not a little unloved, my thoughts returned to the beautiful box of Fuller's Chocolates and Sugars in residence under the stairs. I tried dearly to resist but alas, as my good wife constantly reminds me, "I'm only a man". Thus, I gave in to temptation. I quickly retrieved the chocolates and sitting cosily by the fireside I indulged myself in a Seville Orange Sugar and a Dark Chocolate-covered Cherry. Then again, the sharp dagger of guilt pierced my heart. With sadness I closed the box and once more returned it to its place under the stairs.'

'A week later, while Rachel was out visiting her sister, I had another raid on the unfortunate box of chocolates. I confess that night things got a little out of hand and I ended up finishing the box, except for the Hazelnut Chocolate. Full of remorse and guilt I returned the box to its hiding place.'

'That dear neighbour is how you come to receive a near-empty box. But I urge you to look at it like this. You initially might feel a little hard done by but in fact what you have received is a truly unique gift. Long after your other presents have been forgotten or eaten or thrown out you will have a story, a story you will retell for years and years to come.'

'What did Archie say? The battery is gone in my hearing aid,' said Brenda.

'I'll tell you later darling,' Brenda's husband replied laughing.

'I don't like hazelnut,' wailed the birthday girl.

'Then I might as well be hung for a sheep as a lamb,' I said as my fingers slipped of their own accord around the lone chocolate and I popped it into my mouth.

'We left the house at midnight and as we crossed the Avenue a silvery moon shone brightly in the night sky.'

'That was a pleasant evening,' I said to my good lady as we crossed the Avenue. 'How come you weren't more annoyed about the chocolates?'

'Did you think I didn't know the box was near empty?'

'Why didn't you say something?'

'I wanted to see how you would get out of it.'

'And how did I do?'

'Rachael gave me a devilish smile.'

'Well for a terrible eejit, you did very well.'

CHAPTER 9
PLATFORM NUMBER ONE

The night sky was filled with stars and a bluish-grey light filtered through the living-room window of Number Eleven. The air was heavy with the scent of burning turf. A sod moved in the fireplace and a flicker of sparks spat into the air.

Sitting by the fireside, Millie Ryan waited for her dark-haired, sallow-skinned son, Tim, to tell her what was bothering him. He had been acting strange all evening. One minute he was listening to the radio, the next minute he was staring into space. Now he was sitting at the table reading the evening paper. Then he slapped the paper on the table, rose and strolled into the back garden. His mother observed him through the living-room window. He leaned against the wall, lit a cigarette and watched the plume of grey-blue smoke rise and disappear into the starry night. When he returned to the living room he sat at the table and pretended to read.

Finally, she'd had enough. 'What's the matter with you?' she asked. 'You are like a hen on a hot grill.'

Tim placed the newspaper on the table and sat in the chair on the other side of the fire.

'Murphy's is closing down,' he muttered, staring into the flames.

58

Millie hoped she hadn't heard him right. 'Look at me when you talk to me, son.'

Tim turned to his mother and when she saw the darkness in his eyes she knew she had heard him correctly.

'Next Friday they're closing the carpentry shop for good.'

She grasped at hope. 'You'll find another job.'

'No I won't. We looked everywhere, there are no jobs.'

'Who's "we"?'

'Me and Ronnie.'

'I never liked that Ronnie Quinn. He's two faced.'

'That doesn't matter, Ma.'

'What are you going to do?'

'I have to go to England.'

Despite the heat of the fire, a dread chill swept over Mille. 'No you don't. Your father will find you a job.'

'I've talked to Dad.'

'When?'

'I told him last Thursday when we went for a drink.'

'What did he say?'

'He said he would ask in his factory if there was any work for me but they've told him they're not hiring.'

'Then he's got to keep asking.'

'He has. He plagued his foreman trying to convince him to give me a job. Dad only stopped when the foreman told him in no uncertain terms that he didn't want to hear anymore about his unemployed son. The next day he walked Dublin asking everyone he ever worked for or knew if they had a job for me. No one is hiring.'

'Tim, you can't go to England you're much too young.'

'I'm eighteen, I'm a man.'

'I know you are but you know no one over there. You'll be all on your own.'

'I won't be on my own, Ronnie will be with me.'

'He'll be no help,' said Millie, lowering her voice. 'That lad went missing when they were handing out brains.'

Tim grinned. For a while they sat in silence. Millie thought how fast life went by. Tim was always a skinny little child. She remembered when he was seven and made his First Holy Communion, he was so pleased with himself in his little suit. She smiled when she remembered how he hated shelling peas and cutting the bit of grass in the garden or worst of all helping her make loose yarn into balls of wool. She remembered when he made his Confirmation, he was twelve and again she saw his joyful inquiring eyes beaming with excitement and interest. She remembered when he was thirteen and the look of pride on his face when his school team won the big hurling match. She loved her little boy but now he was a big boy and he was leaving her.

Trying not to show her grief, she said, 'So, when are you and Ronnie planning to go?'

He nodded, clearly relieved by her act of acceptance. 'In ten days, when I get my last pay packet.'

'Will you have enough money?'

'I think so. I'll get a double week and holiday pay. I have a few bob saved. All I need is enough for the boat and train fare and for a place to stay until we find work. Ronnie's older brother lives in London and he said there's lots of work for trained carpentry workers. He said we might even be able to stay in his place for a while.'

'I wouldn't rely on the Quinns for anything. Mrs Quinn is a gossip and all the family are full of talk.' Millie looked at her son and said bravely, 'If you have to go, you have to go, I won't stand in your way. But I want you to remember you always have a home here and you are always welcome. You remember that, son.'

They fell silent again.

The living room door burst open and George, Tim's younger brother, clattered into the room. He stopped when he saw his brother and his mother sitting by the fire.

'I thought no one was home, the place was so quiet.'

'Me and Ma were talking.'

'I'll get the tea ready.' Millie rose and when she reached the kitchen door she stopped. 'Tim has something important to tell you George.'

'Put your hurley away and sit at the fire with me,' Tim said solemnly.

'Everyone is acting strange,' George said, putting the hurley under the stairs. 'Does Ma know about the broken window?'

'No, forget the window. I have something important to tell you.'

'More important than the broken window?' George took the chair opposite his brother. 'You're not going to die are you?'

'No, I'm not going to die but I am going to England.'

'Why are you doing that?'

'The carpentry shop is closing and I have to go away to find work.'

'How long will you be gone?'

'I don't know.'

'A week, a month, a year?'

'George, I don't know but my guess is years.'

'You can't go. I'll miss you.'

'I have to go.'

'Don't go.'

⊨⊩ ⊩⊨

Wearing her light-brown faded woollen overcoat and her Sunday best hat, Millie Ryan scurried head down through the windy Basin on her way home from Mass. Tim was leaving on Tuesday and she was anxious. As she was about to exit the disused reservoir, she met Mrs Quinn.

'I've been meaning to talk to you Mrs Ryan. Can you tell me what the arrangements are for next Tuesday? My Ronnie tells me nothing.' Mrs Quinn removed the wind-ruffled scarf from her head and ran her fingers through her thinning hair. 'Everyone wants to know what's happening.'

'I don't know the everyone you're talking about and if your son won't tell you his arrangements maybe he has his reasons.'

'Is that all the thanks I get for keeping you informed?'

'You don't keep me informed. You gossip,' Millie snapped and stormed away from a stunned Mrs Quinn.

Tim's father, Joe Ryan was a tall man with big hands, a thin moustache and sallow skin. He was a quiet man who cared greatly for his two boys. On the night before Tim's departure he brought his son to Conway's pub and handed him a crumpled envelope. Tim opened the envelope and was stunned to see two five pound notes.

'Dad this is too much. I can't take it. It's more than two weeks of your wages.'

'Take it. You'll need every penny of it and promise me if you run out of money, you'll write to me. I want you to promise you'll do that.'

'I will Dad, I promise.'

'Good. I wish you weren't going. It's breaking your mother's heart and it's not doing mine much good. But what has to be has to be. Now, let's have a pint.'

On the day of his departure, a sombre Tim stepped out of the house and looked up and down the Avenue. Struggling with Tim's suitcase, young George staggered out the front door behind him.

'I'll take that,' Joe said to his youngest son. 'Go talk to Tim.'

'Where's Ronnie? Why is he not here?' Millie asked her son as they set off down the Avenue.

'He's gone to Cabra to say goodbye to his Granny. He's meeting us at the train station.'

When they arrived, the train was waiting on Platform One. Sad-faced people were moving silently about murmuring goodbye to each other. Tim looked along the platform for his friend.

'I don't see Ronnie or any of the Quinns,' said Mr Ryan

'He'll be here. He's just a bit late.'

'He's more than a bit late. The train's leaving in a few minutes.' Mr Ryan ran his finger along his thin moustache.

Two minutes later the only people standing on the platform were the train guard and the Ryan family. The guard walked along the platform, closing the third-class compartment doors.

'Are you boarding? The train has to leave,' the guard said to Tim,

Tim could not think, he felt numb. He felt a hot burning rage in the pit of his stomach; he had believed in his friend and his friend had let him down. He didn't know what to do. He felt utterly alone. He looked up and down the platform once more. No Ronnie. He looked at his father and his mother and his brother and he made up his mind. He was going to have to go to England on his own. He embraced his father and brother, kissed his mother and stepped into the train carriage.

The guard closed the door behind him, and unfurled his green flag.

Mr Ryan sighed, George sniffled and Millie's eyes filled with tears. The guard waved the flag. The train released a great cloud of steam and smoke and, chugging loudly, disappeared into the mist and the night.

CHAPTER 10
VISITORS TO THE AVENUE

The Avenue had many visitors, the noisiest of which were the red-faced, cap-wearing farmers who drove their cows down the Avenue on their way to the cattle market. The far-away clattering of hooves announced their imminent arrival, sending the residents of the Avenue racing to close their parlour windows and front doors. Within minutes confused cows poked their huge heads into any open window or door. Loud-voiced cattlemen in old woollen overcoats tied with súgán rope walloped the bewildered creatures with sticks. As soon as the cows were gone, front doors flew open and housewives with buckets and spades descended on the heaps of dung the cattle had deposited on their Avenue. Later that day the precious droppings were used as fertiliser in the women's small back gardens.

There were other colourful visitors to the Avenue. The ragman with his donkey and cart was a great friend to all the children. In exchange for old clothes, he would give a delighted child a small toy or an inexpensive knick-knack.

Mr Stanley, 'the pig man,' was the children's true favourite. He was a kind, good-natured man who arrived with his horse and cart to collect potato peelings, cabbage stalks, stale bread and other kitchen scraps to feed to his pigs. As he waited for his clients to bring out their buckets, Mr Stanley would smooth and caress his horse's neck or comb her mane. One day young Johnny Farrell, the little fellow who lived in Number Thirty One, asked Mr Stanley if he could feed the horse a carrot. Mr Stanley nodded and Johnny held up the vegetable to the animal's mouth. The horse's huge teeth gripped the carrot, chomped on it and swallowed it. Mesmerised, young Johnny stared at the enormous animal as she shook her head and the polished buckles on her harness jingled musically. When Mr Stanley and his horse and cart arrived the following week, young Paul O'Sullivan and a few other children were standing with Johnny waiting to feed the animal. Young O'Sullivan was about to give the horse a small turnip when his mother shouted from her front door, 'Paul O'Sullivan, don't you dare feed our dinner to that animal.'

Early every morning an unseen milkman from Merville or HB Dairies left a bottle or bottles of milk on the doorstep of each house and every Friday evening, except on Good Friday, the milkmen collected their money. In the afternoons breadmen from Boland's or Kennedy's Bakeries left turnovers or loaves or sliced pans on the windowsills.

In autumn and winter the coalmen arrived and delivered coal and slack to the people of The Avenue. Black-faced men with coal-dust encrusted caps and coal sacks draped across their backs drove their lorries or horses and carts up the Avenue. Shouting 'co-ell and slack for sale' the men knocked on the doors and delivered bags of coal or slack.

The insurance man was another regular. In the 1950s it was a matter of honour for older people to have enough money 'for me burial'. So every month the older residents of the Avenue handed their insurance man a shilling for a policy that would, eventually, pay for their funeral.

But the most exciting and the most eagerly awaited visitor to the Avenue was the gasman. Each house had a gas meter. To keep a constant supply of gas to a house the meter had to be fed a shilling or two every day. The meter, usually located in the living room under the stairs, filled up quickly so it needed to be emptied regularly. Every six weeks or so a man from the gas company visited each house and emptied the money from the meter. The excitement began when word went around the houses that the gasman had been seen in the neighbourhood. When the gasman knocked on the front door of a family home the excitement turned into joyous anticipation. Carrying a huge leather bag the gasman greeted the woman of the house and entered. From the steps of the stairs the children of the house watched the man unlock the meter, remove the money box and carry it to the living room table. There he would remove a green felt cloth from his bag, spread it on the table and empty the contents of the money box onto the felt. The gasman would then stack the shillings in tens until all the money was counted. By now the children's excitement was at fever pitch. The gasman checked the meter and calculated the amount owed. He returned to the table, placed the outstanding amount in small paper bags and put the paper bags in his big leather bag. The great moment was now at hand. The gasman handed the remaining shillings on his green cloth to the woman of the house as a rebate.

When the gas man departed the woman of the house would give each child a sixpence or three-penny bit, depending on the size of the rebate, to spend on whatever they chose. Yes, the gasman was easily the most exciting visitor to the Avenue.

CHAPTER 11

LETTERS

Part 1

Victoria Lyons was an exceptionally beautiful, intelligent young woman who had a great passion for singing. She had first auditioned for the Pro-cathedral Choir when she was ten years old, and after three years of auditioning was finally accepted. She loved to stand in the midst of the sea of voices and let the waves of sound transport her to a special magical place. The first Sunday morning she sang solo with the choir was the happiest day of her life.

Yet despite Victoria's singing talent, everyone she met told her how pretty she was and so she came to believe being beautiful was all that she had to be to succeed in the world.

Victoria had only just turned eighteen when Aiden Sweeney first asked her out. One bright August day, he waited at the bottom of the Avenue for nearly an hour for her to return home from her job in the New Ireland Assurance Company office, in Dawson Street.

He saw her rushing up the Avenue. The closer she got the more nervous Aiden became. When she was ten feet from him he adjusted his tie and, summoning all his courage, stepped out in front of her. Caught by surprise, Victoria stumbled and skittered off the footpath.

'Would you like to go to the pictures?' Aiden asked, exactly as he had rehearsed it.

'Idiot, why did you step in front of me like that? You could have killed me.'

'I'm sorry.' He was standing so close to her, he could smell the perfumed soap on her skin. 'What about the pictures?'

'Pictures? Are you asking me to go to an art exhibition?'

'N..No?' he stammered, confused.

'You said you wanted to take me to the pictures?'

'Oh, I meant the films, the Carlton Cinema.'

'I don't go to a particular cinema, I go to see a specific film,' she said as she walked on.

'We could go to any film you liked,' Aiden said, following her up the Avenue.

Victoria stopped. 'I know you, don't I? You're in the parish choir. You're a tenor.'

'You like singing too, don't you? ' Aiden replied, thinking his chances of a date had improved. 'Does that mean you'll go with me to the pictures?'

'No, you're a tradesman. I never go out with tradesmen.'

'I am not a tradesman, I am an apprentice carpenter.'

'Is that supposed to impress me?'

He looked at her, hard. 'You're a snob. I don't think I want to go out with you after all.'

'Dear me, I wonder how I'll get over the disappointment,' Victoria replied and left Aiden standing on the Avenue.

Many young men invited Victoria to the cinema, theatre, dress dances and about every social gathering imaginable. Most invitations she rejected out of hand; a few were accepted but fewer were given the honour of a second outing. Victoria was a flirt and was indiscreet when talking about her suitors. She was engaged twice, once to Richard Burke, a shop owner in Phibsboro, and once to Brian McEnroe, a clerk in a shipping company. Both engagements were terminated unceremoniously by the cool, beautiful girl.

'Men are like buses, there'll be another along in a minute,' her mother used to say.

━≼╫╪≻━

Twenty-three years ago, Victoria's mother Henrietta had married a successful businessman Richard Lyons and they lived in a beautiful seafront house in Clontarf.

'When fate took my husband and left me a widow, it was life's cruellest blow.'

With little income, except for a small pension, she cursed heaven and declared herself disgusted with God, Ireland and mankind. She sold the beautiful home in Clontarf and moved into a more affordable if more modest accommodation: Number Nineteen on the Avenue.

Victoria had no recollection of her father. During her years of growing up Victoria often fantasised about her father. She imagined whole conversations with him, the places he might have taken her and things they might have done together.

━≼╫╪≻━

Aiden Sweeney left school at fourteen to be apprenticed as a carpenter in the Granby Lane Joinery. He showed such skill and enthusiasm for woodwork that by the age of twenty one he was one of Dublin's most in-demand furniture restorers. If carpentry was Aiden's first love, singing was his second. All through his apprenticeship he had remained a member of the parish choir.

On his twenty-first birthday, Aiden was invited by the choirmaster of the Pro-cathedral Choir, Dr Henry Wilson, to join as one of its principal singers. Aiden was so delighted he took his parents, John and Mary Sweeney, to Marco's fish and chipper for a sit-down meal to celebrate.

Dressed in a three-piece tweed suit, yellow shirt and check bow tie Dr Wilson was introducing Aiden to the assembled choir when an out-of-breath Victoria burst into the choir room.

'Sorry I'm late. I got delayed in work,' Victoria said. She tipped her head to one side and flashed her eyes shyly at the choirmaster.

'Don't let it happen again,' the choirmaster said and glared disapprovingly at her. 'Now where was I? Oh yes, I was introducing Mr Sweeney, our new lead tenor.'

'A new tenor? The choir doesn't need a new tenor?' Victoria said loudly to her friend Peggy.

Dr Wilson glared. 'Miss Lyons, your comments are ungracious, rude and uncalled for. If you ever again speak negatively about a decision of mine, I will ask for your resignation. Do I make myself clear?' All eyes turned to Victoria and she nodded sheepishly. 'Now, apologise to Mr Sweeney.'

'I apologise,' she said, under her breath.

'I didn't quite hear that Miss Lyons.'

'I apologise,' Victoria said more loudly.

An hour later when the choir took a break, a still-annoyed Victoria approached Aiden.

'Did you join the choir in the hope I might go out with you?'

'Oh, that's who you are, I thought I recognised you. No, I joined the choir because Dr Wilson invited me to join.'

'You were invited to join the choir?'

'Yes, isn't everyone?'

'No, they are not,' Victoria replied and walked away in a huff.

Every Thursday evening, Aiden and his best friend David Halpin played billiards in the Dorset Street Billiard's Hall. One evening after their game they stopped in Marco's fish and chipper and were standing waiting to order when the pretty Ruth O'Casey and her friend Peggy Tierney waltzed into the chipper.

Aiden nudged David. 'Hello Ruth, you can go ahead of us if you like,' he said, smiling at the girls.

'No you're grand, you go ahead,' replied Ruth.

'We insist,' Aiden said with a bow and a wave of his hand.

'Very well,' Ruth said and she sauntered past them to the counter and ordered two one-and-ones.

Aiden whispered to David and he nodded in agreement.

'Would you two ladies be interested in going to the pictures with us on Saturday night?' asked Aiden.

The girls looked at each other.

'We might,' Ruth replied with a giggle and the two girls left the chipper.

━━◁┼▷━━

Dr Henry Wilson approached Victoria in the choir loft before Sunday Mass and asked if he might have a word.

'I am about to ask our new lead tenor Mr Sweeney to sing the Gloria hymn on Sunday.'

Victoria's response came like a burst of gunfire.

'But I always sing the Gloria hymn.'

'True. But I do want Aiden to sing a solo. He has such a beautiful voice.'

'But it's my solo.'

'Victoria, we will find another solo for you, perhaps something at Christmas.'

That's eight months away, Victoria wanted to say, but she didn't. Instead she forced a smile which belied the stony gaze in her eyes.

⚊⟨⟩⚊

Two months later Victoria celebrated her twenty-first birthday by inviting a small group of female friends to a party in her home. They crammed into the parlour. The Lyons' home was the same size as every other house in the terrace but its sofas, coffee table, dining table, chairs and curtains were all designed for the house in Clontarf. Number Nineteen looked as if it had shrunk around its contents.

During the evening everyone had to perform a party piece; Ann Byrne sang an Irish ballad, *The Butcher Boy*, Maggie Toomey recited a poem and Joan Doyle played the piano. When it came to Ruth O'Casey's turn she offered to give a tarot card reading and Victoria graciously accepted the offer. Maggie lit a candle, Joan turned off the light and the girls gathered around the card table. Ruth slowly turned over six tarot cards, leaned forward and quickly gathered the cards up again.

'Why did you do that?' asked Victoria. 'What did the cards say?'

'Victoria, this is a party game and I'm not really a fortune teller.'

'I know, but what did the cards say?'

'I can't tell you. I don't know enough about card reading.'

'I insist. Tell me what you know.'

Ruth looked at the card table and spoke softly. 'The cards say you'll never marry.'

'I'll die an old maid?'

'That's what the cards said.'

'You don't think I can get a man?'

'No! Victoria, I don't think that.'

'There isn't a fellow around here who hasn't asked me out.'

Ruth shrugged her shoulders, saying nothing.

'Did the cards tell you your new boyfriend Aiden once asked me out?'

'Victoria, this is a parlour game. Don't take it so seriously.'

'You don't believe me, do you, Ruth?'

'I don't care if he asked you out or not.'

Ruth returned the cards to their box.

'Victoria, it's a game, who believes in fortune-telling?' interjected Joan Doyle.

'You're right Joan. It is a silly game. Let's play some proper cards.'

At the end of the evening when Victoria was helping Ruth with her coat she leaned close and whispered, 'Say goodbye to your boyfriend.'

Ruth stared at Victoria. 'What did you say?'

'Oh don't look so shocked. I was only joking. Don't take everything so seriously.'

⚓

On Friday night Ruth asked Aiden if he ever asked Victoria out on a date and his reaction surprised her; he laughed.

'I did yea, a long time ago and do you know what she said to me?'

Ruth shook her head.

'She said she didn't go out with tradesmen.'

'And what did you say?'

'I told her I didn't go out with snobs. No, I didn't say that, but I told her she was a snob.'

'How come you never told me that?'

'It was years ago, long before we started to go out together.'

'You see a lot of her, don't you? I mean at choir practice and all?'

'I suppose so.'

'Would you still like to go out with her?'

'No I wouldn't.' Aiden put his arm around Ruth. 'I think you are being a bit silly.'

Ruth shrugged off his arm. 'I'm not being silly.'

'Where's all this is coming from?'

'You still like her.'

'I never said that.'

'But it's true.'

'No, it's not.'

Ruth stormed away. The following day when Aiden asked her to go to the pictures she refused. And he didn't ask her again.

✦

After a particularly long and tedious choir practice, Victoria approached Aiden and suggested he join her for a cup of coffee. Aiden looked suspiciously at her and she coyly lowered her head.

'I have something important to tell you.'

As she led him up the stairs of the busy Rainbow Café, the soft voice of Nat King Cole filled the room. A group of young people were standing around the illuminated jukebox, talking and swaying to the music; others were sitting chatting while still more drifted aimlessly around the café. A table by a window overlooking O'Connell Street became vacant and Aiden and Victoria took it. Aiden removed his cap and stuffed it into his pocket, then ordered coffee for both of them. Victoria rested her elbows on the table, placed her chin in her hands and gazed intently at him.

'What's so important?' Aiden asked, leaning back in his chair.

'I think we got off on the wrong foot,' she said, and tucked a loose strand of hair behind her ear. 'I'm sorry if I wasn't more welcoming to you when you first joined the choir.'

'Oh that's alright, you were just being you.'

'What is that supposed to mean?'

'You're snobby, that's all.'

'That is not true.'

'Victoria, you said you had something important to tell me?'

'Yes I do.' Victoria looked around the café and when she was sure she would not be overheard, she said, 'I don't believe the rumour that Ruth was going out with Paddy Albright on the nights you were at choir practice.'

'What? I never heard that. Why are you talking to me about Ruth? Ruth is not your business. I'm not comfortable having this conversation.'

'I understand,' Victoria said, as if she had been crushed by Aiden's remark.

Aiden stood. 'This was a mistake.'

'Could we at least drink the coffee we ordered?'

'No,' Aiden replied; he dropped enough money on the table for the coffees, and left.

Victoria was astonished; no one had ever treated her like that before.

⟞⟝⟞⟝⟞

When Ruth learned that Aiden and Victoria had been seen together in the Rainbow Café she was furious. She stormed down the Avenue and knocked loudly on Victoria's front door.

'I'd like to talk to Victoria,' Ruth said when Mrs Lyons answered the door.

'Come in, Ruth. I believe Victoria is upstairs.' Henrietta always spoke as if the house was a mansion of many rooms. 'I'll go and find her.'

Ruth sat in the parlour and waited for what seemed forever. She looked around the room and wondered at the oversized furniture.

'I know this is all a game to you, Victoria, but it's not to me,' she said when Victoria finally joined her. 'I love Aiden and so keep away from him.'

'I've no idea what you're talking about. As far as I know, you and Aiden are not seeing each other. All Aiden and I did was have a coffee, we had choir business to talk about. Now, if you don't mind, I was in the middle of something.'

＞＜

The following Wednesday when Victoria arrived for choir practice, Dr Wilson asked for a word.

'The other night while I was having my steak and kidney pie, Mrs Wilson reminded me that when we were in the Vatican some years ago, we heard the Gloria hymn sung as a near-duet. It occurred to me that it might be a good idea if you and Aiden sang the Gloria together on Easter Sunday. He would be the lead voice of course and you would support him in some of the harmonies. What do you think? Good idea?'

'It's a wonderful idea,' Victoria replied with a closed-lip smile.

'Good, don't say anything to Aiden, I want it to be a surprise. I'm waiting for the sheet music to arrive from Rome, so not a word.'

Victoria went into the ladies and silently screamed.

＞＜

To Victoria's great surprise her voice blended beautifully with Aiden's, their breathing matched, they sang at an equal level, almost as one voice. Dr Wilson was delighted. After the choir practice, Victoria asked Aiden if he'd go for coffee to the Rainbow Café again with her.

'No, not a good idea,' he said.

'Please, I want to apologise to you by buying you a coffee. I didn't realise what a wonderful voice you have.'

'Alright, but I won't go to the Rainbow Café with you. The Palm Grove in O'Connell Street is my limit.'

They were sitting waiting on their coffee to arrive when a well-dressed, middle-aged man stood up in the back of the cafe and, with a slight limp, crossed to their table.

'Victoria Lyons?' he inquired when he reached them.

'Yes,' Victoria replied, with a frown.

The stranger's face lit up. 'Born in Clontarf? Your mother is called Henrietta? You are the image of her.'

'I don't know you. Who are you?'

The man leaned on his silver-tipped walking stick. 'Don't you recognise me? I sent you many photos over the years.'

Victoria's voice rose in alarm. 'What are you talking about? I don't know you and I think you should go away.'

'I'm your father, the man who has been writing to you every birthday and Christmas since you were three years old.'

'My father's dead.'

The man was clearly shocked. 'Is that what Henrietta told you?'

'Sir, I insist you leave,' interjected Aiden. 'If you don't, I'll call the manager.'

'Victoria, what has your mother told you about me?'

'You are not my father,' Victoria said with such intensity that the other diners in the café turned and stared at her. 'Go away. I don't want to talk to you.'

The man stepped back. 'At least I know now why you never answered my letters. I wish you well, Victoria. Nice meeting you, young man.' He handed Aiden his business card. 'Look after my daughter, treat her better than I did.'

'Yes, I will,' Aiden replied, not knowing what else to say.

Richard Lyons placed his trilby on his head, touched its brim and walked slowly out of the café. Victoria felt light-headed and the room swirled around her. Aiden quickly went around the table to sit beside her; he put his arm around her and held her.

'Will you walk me home?' she asked, pale-faced.

'Of course I will, and we don't have to talk if you don't want to.'

A sharp wind whispered through the trees as they exited the café. Without exchanging a word they made their way up O'Connell Street and through North Frederick Street and when they reached Number Nineteen, they stopped.

'I haven't always been nice to you Aiden and I'm sorry. I have no right to ask anything of you but please don't tell anyone about that awful man and the ridiculous claims he made.'

'I'll tell no one about him, he is nobody's business but yours. Also, I want you to know I intend to make up with Ruth so I don't think we should go for coffee again.' Aiden started to move away, stopped and with a grin added, 'I don't think my heart could take it.'

A trace of a smile formed on Victoria's lips.

LETTERS

Part 2

Victoria removed her coat and collapsed into an armchair in front of the dying embers of a fire. She was disappointed her mother had not waited up. She wanted to talk to her. She wanted to tell her all about the madman in the café.

Or was he mad? Was there even the remotest chance he was her father? She thought about the one wedding photograph in the house, which she'd found in the back of her mother's wardrobe. It was an old picture, from over twenty years ago. Richard Lyons had been young and handsome, with a full head of black hair. The man in the café was silver-haired, with a limp.

She went to bed but she couldn't sleep. She kept pushing thoughts of the man out of her mind but they refused to go; they kept returning, over and over until she fell asleep and then she dreamt about him.

At breakfast when Victoria told her mother about the man in the café, Henrietta reacted with fury.

'Your father is dead,' she barked, rattling the crockery as she slammed the teapot on the table.

'I know, Mother. I was just wondering what he died of. Where is he buried?'

'Why do you want to know that rubbish? Do you want to put flowers on his grave? Perhaps you'd like to have a Mass said for his black soul?'

'His black soul?' Victoria was horrified. Her mother had always bewailed becoming a widow.

'There are things I have never told you, and I won't be telling you now.'

'Mother, there's no need to get so upset. I'm only asking simple questions.'

'Dreadful questions, selfish questions, questions you should not be asking.'

'Where is my father's grave?'

'Glasnevin Cemetery and don't ask me where in the cemetery.'

⋙⊣⊢⋘

Carrying a small bouquet of flowers, Aiden Sweeney walked into a newly refurbished Pims Department Store. He stopped at the information desk and asked to speak to Miss Ruth O'Casey in the general office. Dressed in a black skirt, white blouse and a small string of pearls around her neck, an intrigued Ruth rushed onto the shop floor. When she saw Aiden her eyes widened. When he handed her the flowers and asked if they could meet after work, she beamed with delight.

'Miss O'Casey you are aware company policy forbids personal visitors, please ask your friend to leave,' said the manager, Mr Oliver Martin, as he picked invisible hairs off the sleeves of his suit jacket.

'Mr Martin, I will ask my friend to leave but first I have to tell you, he is more than a friend, he is my boyfriend and I am going to kiss him and then return to work. Feel free to watch or close your eyes,' Ruth said, and she kissed Aiden firmly on the lips.

Mr Martin closed his eyes.

━┼┼━

Early the following Saturday morning, Victoria walked through Glasnevin Cemetery's iron gates, past ancient gravestones with their beards of lichen and into the cemetery's grey administration building. She informed the desk clerk that she had an appointment with a Mr Tony O'Connell. She was aimlessly turning the pages of an old magazine in the waiting area when the short, fat, middle-aged Tony O'Connell caught sight of Victoria through the office window. He checked his reflection in the glass window, patted down his hair and quickly approached his client.

'Good afternoon,' Mr O'Connell said, as he gave Victoria what he considered a roguish wink. 'I have your enquiry form about your late father's grave but I am sorry to tell you we have no record of a burial of a Richard Lyons in the month of the year you stated on the form. I also checked the previous year and the subsequent year, all without success. Perhaps your father is buried in another cemetery.'

━┼┼━

The following Monday, Victoria sat in the main office of New Ireland Assurance Company in Dawson Street still thinking about what to say to her mother. She jumped when the office manager's chubby hand slapped hard on her desk.

'Oh, Mr Finch, what's the matter?'

'That's the question I want you to answer. The company doesn't pay you to daydream. Please attend to your work.'

'Sorry Mr Finch,' Victoria said and resumed typing a letter to a Kerry farmer rejecting his claim for storm damage to one of his out-houses.

The instant Mr Finch returned to his office Victoria's mind returned to thoughts of the non-existent grave, and the unanswered letters that the strange man in the cafe talked about.

When she returned home that night, her mother was sitting by the fire. Victoria sat opposite her.

'Mother, I went to Glasnevin Cemetery at the weekend. There is no record of father being buried there.'

Her mother went pale. 'Why can't you leave things alone?'

'I can't leave things alone. A stranger came up to me and said he was my father and now I learn my father is not buried where you said he was buried, what am I supposed to think?'

'I don't know who the man you met was, but I can assure you that your father is dead to me.' Her mother pulled out a lace handkerchief and mopped her eyes vigorously.

Victoria sat up straight.

'"Dead to you"? What in heaven's name does that mean?'

'If you must know, your father deserted me and ran off to Wales with a floozy.'

Victoria's mouth fell open. 'What?'

'He didn't tell you that did he? I thought not. He deserted me, disgraced me, shamed me and left me to raise you on my own.'

'What happened to the letters he wrote to me?'

Henrietta paused a moment. She crushed the lace handkerchief in her right hand. 'He never wrote you any letters.'

'He said he wrote to me.'

'Your father is incapable of telling the truth. He never wrote a single letter to you, he lied to me, cheated on me and now he's lying to you.'

Aiden and Ruth resumed seeing each other. For a while everything went well. Ruth was happy, even delighted, with the return of her boyfriend but Aiden soon began to have second thoughts. Ruth was charming, honest and pretty, but Aiden wasn't enjoying the time he spent with her, he often felt bored, sometimes he even felt annoyed, but what concerned him most was he could not stop thinking about Victoria.

On Saturday night Ruth, Aiden, Peggy and David were in the National Ballroom dancing to the music of the Clipper Carltons. The ballroom was crowded and when the band took a break, Aiden suggested they should go for a mineral.

'I don't know if I feel like a mineral,' Ruth said.

'For heaven's sake Victoria, it's only a mineral, we're not planning a holiday together,' said Aiden.

Peggy, David and Ruth stared at Aiden.

'What's wrong?' asked Aiden.

'Nothing's wrong, at least it wouldn't be if my name was Victoria,' Ruth said and stormed off to the ladies.

'Aiden sometimes you can be very stupid,' Peggy said and rushed after her friend.

'You dropped yourself right in it there,' David said with a grin.

'Damn it David, this is not funny. What am I going to do?'

'You'll have to apologise, a lot.'

Aiden waited and the moment Ruth exited the ladies he approached her and told her he was sorry. She graciously accepted his apology but no matter how hard she tried, Ruth could not get the incident out of her mind.

━◁╫▷━

Aiden was in the workshop working on a carving that formed part of a mahogany sideboard when he stopped, placed his chisel on the workbench and went into the workshop yard. Leaning against the wall he thought about Ruth and what she said to him when they walked home from the dance.

'Are you sure you want to continue seeing me? I want you to be my boyfriend but you have to want it too. I don't want to be some sort of a pity girlfriend.'

'You're not a pity girlfriend, whatever that means. I have no interest in Victoria,' Aiden tried to assure her, but they both knew he was not telling the truth.

—≺+≻—

When Ruth answered the door and saw the expression on Aiden's face she felt a chill that had nothing to do with the weather.

'Ruth, I need to talk to you,' Aiden said with great seriousness.

'Come in,' Ruth replied and brought him into the parlour.

'I don't know how to put this without hurting you...' Aiden began.

'You're breaking up with me, aren't you?'

'Err, yes. I suppose I am.'

'There is no supposing. What did I do wrong?'

'You did nothing wrong. I think we're just not right for each other.'

'When did you decide that?'

'That's unimportant.'

'This is about Victoria?'

'This has nothing to do with Victoria. It is between you and me.'

'Like hell it is, I'm not a fool and don't treat me like one. Let me tell you something about your precious Victoria, she will never be yours, she'll never be anyone's. She's a beautiful, unfeeling, empty vessel.'

'I'm sorry, I know this is hurtful.'

'I haven't finished. This is the second time you've broken up with me. There will not be a third. Now please leave.'

'I'm sorry...'
'Leave.'

⊱✦⊰

If her mother had kept that one wedding photo in the box at the back of her wardrobe, maybe she'd kept other mementos? Henrietta had gone to buy butter from Moore's corner shop, and Victoria sat on her mother's oversized bed in the empty house. The room smelt of Eau de Cologne and Vick's Rub and looked like a hurricane had torn through it. Her mother's kimono-style silk dressing gown lay carelessly strewn across the quilt. At last, she made her decision and began her search.

Under the box in the wardrobe was another bigger box, containing a wedding veil and lace gloves. And under the veil was a collection of letters tied with a ribbon.

Victoria untied the letters. They were addressed to her.

Henrietta was back home and sitting by the fire writing in her diary when Victoria took the armchair opposite her. Without a word she held out the letters. Her mother glanced momentarily at them and resumed her writing.

'You had no right to keep them from me,' said Victoria.

'I had every right. He deserted us and never gave a care for what happened to you.'

'In his letters, he says he loves me.'

'Words are cheap. Actions are a more reliable guide to people than words.'

'He sent money every month for my upkeep.'

'A meagre pittance.'

'Mam, I have a half-brother and a half-sister!'

'I don't want to hear about them, Victoria.'

'Maybe you don't. But you had no right to keep his letters from me.'

'Perhaps I was wrong,' Henrietta said unconvincingly. 'Victoria, I did what I thought was best. Don't paint me the villain.'

'Did you not think of my feelings?'

'What feelings are those? Victoria, we are so alike.'

'No we're not,' Victoria said, staring at her mother. 'And why does my father call me "airy" in his letters?'

'That was a silliness of his. When you were young, you had difficulty saying the word fairy, you pronounced it airy, so he adopted your way of saying it, then he began to call you "his little airy", such silliness.'

Victoria didn't think it was silly.

⚊⟨⊹⟩⚊

It was Saturday night and Aiden was enjoying the sing-along in the Abbey Tavern with an unusually silent David Halpin.

'Are you alright?' Aiden asked his friend during a quiet moments between songs.

David looked away and rubbed his chin. 'There is something I want to ask you. I asked Ruth out on a date and she said yes. Is that alright with you?'

'Of course, it's alright with me. If Ruth wants to go out with you, that's her business and you don't need my permission. 'But I wonder why she's lowering her standards.' David shrugged and Aiden grinned. 'I never knew you fancied Ruth?'

'Neither did I,' David said with another shrug.

⚊⟨⊹⟩⚊

Laying in bed Victoria thought about how many of her boyfriends she had really liked. Very few, if any. She remembered the oddities, the fellow with the huge feet and the one who cried at the opera and the two fellows she had been engaged to, Brian and

Richard. She hadn't loved either of her fiancés, she certainly didn't enjoy kissing them and their advances were annoying; both were so clingy. She straightened the covers under her chin.

Am I really like my mother? I've never had romantic dreams. I've never fallen in love. I've never felt the passion or the ecstasy poets write about. I wonder why?

The wind rattled the open window, she pushed back the covers, jumped out of bed and slammed the window closed. She returned to bed, turned on her side and fell into a restless sleep.

At choir practice Aiden made a point of avoiding Victoria. During every break, he managed to be on the opposite side of the room and the moment choir practice was over he grabbed his coat and left. One night when Aiden rushed out, it was raining so hard he had to stop and shelter in the church porch.

'You're keeping your distance from me' Victoria said, joining him.

Aiden didn't reply but flipped up the collar of his overcoat.

'Can we talk? There is something I need to discuss with you.'

'Is this something about that man in the café?'

'Yes.'

Aiden made a point of looking at his watch.

'I don't have much time. Let's go to the Palm Grove Café, it's the closest.'

Before Aiden had finished speaking Victoria opened her umbrella and walked out into the lashing rain. When they arrived at the café it was almost empty. Victoria chose a table near the door and as she closed her umbrella she saw Ruth and David sitting at a table in the back of the café. Victoria tugged Aiden's sleeve and glanced at his friends. He looked over and when he caught David's eye, he smiled.

'Want to say hello?' asked Aiden.

'No, I'm sure Ruth doesn't want to talk to me.'

'I'll say a quick hello.'

'Do you have to?'

'I'm not going to pretend they are not here.'

Victoria sat and watched Aiden approach his friends. She admired the ease with which he interacted with his ex-girlfriend and best friend. She watched how they talked and smiled at each other and, when Aiden said goodbye, how he touched Ruth affectionately on the shoulder.

'It's their third date, they were at the pictures, sorry "the cinema",' Aiden said as he returned to their table. 'Now, what did you want to tell me?'

Victoria leaned forward and spoke in a near whisper.

'The man was telling the truth. He is my father. I found his letters. He wrote a letter to me every Christmas and every year on my birthday.'

He stared at her. 'Are you sure?'

'Yes, I don't know what to do.'

'Are you going to contact him?'

'I don't know. My mother says they change nothing, my father is still the man who deserted us.'

'What do you mean, they change nothing? They change everything. Your mother lied to you and hid the letters that were yours. Your father is alive and he wants to get to know you. Did you ever think it wasn't you he deserted?'

'He deserted my mother and me,' snapped Victoria. 'And even if it was my mother he left, it still wasn't the right thing to do.'

'What would have been the right thing to do?'

'Stop asking me awkward questions.'

'You should be asking yourself those questions, not feeling guilty because you read your father's letters and they made you feel good.'

'I never said they made me feel good.'

'Not in so many words.'

'There is something else. He's written to me again, and this time I got to the postman first. He wants to meet with me and talk.'

'What do you want to do?'

'I don't know, will you come with me?'

Richard Lyons sat in a quiet corner of the Wintergarden Lounge in the Gresham Hotel and waited nervously on his daughter's arrival. He had arrived early and had spent the time thinking about what he would say to her. Ever since he laid eyes on her in the café nearly a month ago he had longed to talk to her and learn more about her.

When she entered the lounge with her young man, his heart jumped. He stood so quickly that a stab of pain in his arthritic knee made him flinch.

'Delighted you came,' he said as they arrived at his table.

He held out his hand but Victoria did not accept it.

'I'm here to listen to what you have to say,' she announced, and sat as far away from him as she could.

Richard turned to Aiden. 'Nice to see you again, I don't believe we were introduced properly last time we met. I'm Richard Lyons and you are?'

'Aiden Sweeney.'

Aiden shook Richard's hand. 'Nice to meet you Mr Lyons.'

'Would you both like some tea?'

'No thank you,' Victoria said curtly.

'How shall we begin?' Richard asked, sitting and rubbing his throbbing knee. 'Victoria, what would you like to ask me?'

Victoria placed her hands on her lap. 'Did you leave Dublin with another woman?'

'Yes, her name is Helen. I loved her and I still love her. As I wrote to you, we have two children, Sally and Tom. So you have a brother and a sister.'

'A half-brother and half-sister,' corrected Victoria. 'Why did you desert my mother and me?'

'I left because she didn't love me. I never meant to hurt you but the situation with your mother was so painful I didn't feel I had another choice. I know I can't hope to share in your life but I want you to know I loved you and I never stopped thinking about you.'

'Anything else?' Victoria asked coldly.

'Yes, I've written you another letter, it's different from the others; perhaps you'll read it.'

Richard took the letter from his pocket and tried to give it to her.

'I have no interest in your letter. I'd like to go now, Aiden,' she said and walked towards the door. Aiden stood.

'If you like I'll take the letter and give it to Victoria at another time.'

'Would you? Do you think she'll read it?'

'Yes, she read all your other letters. They are important to her.'

Richard breathed deep and a smile spread across his face.

The city was steeped in long shadows as Victoria and Aiden walked home in near silence. When they reached Number Nineteen, Aiden reached into his pocket and held out the letter.

'I said I wasn't interested in it.'

'I know, but you are interested.'

'You think you know me?'

'I do know you, a little.'

Victoria leaned over, kissed Aiden on the cheek, took the letter and said goodnight.

LETTERS

Part 3

Dear Victoria,

No one fully understands why they do things or why they behave in certain ways. The decisions I made concerning your mother and you were not random or vindictive but complex and deeply personal.

When your mother and I married, I thought our love would last a lifetime. But I was wrong, very wrong. I never really understood your mother. The woman I married was different from the woman I thought I married. She showed no interest in me, and I was unhappy and lonely. I felt I didn't have a partner, at least one that shared my views, hopes and dreams. I felt trapped, lost and alone. Then I met Helen and I saw life held other possibilities. I dared to believe I could be happy and after much thought, I made my decision to leave. It was a heart-breaking decision but I made it.

The night I left for Wales, I went into your bedroom and looked on your sleeping self and my heart shattered. I kissed your forehead and left. Every day of my life I have thought about you and every night I prayed for you and wondered what I lost by leaving you. Do not blame your mother for what happened, it is I who is to blame.

I was not there for you as you grew up but I can be there for you in the future if you want me to be. If ever you need someone to talk to or if there is anything, anything at all I can do for you, don't hesitate to ask. It would be my honour to help.

Think kindly of me.

Your father,
Richard.

Victoria placed her father's letter on her dressing table and tears flowed down her cheeks.

⚊⚊

Sitting beneath the Harry Clark stained glass windows in Bewley's Café on Grafton Street, Henrietta tapped her foot against the table leg. Her daughter was late; another slight.

'Sorry I'm late,' Victoria said as she slipped into the seat opposite.

'What kept you?'

'A girl in the office asked me to pick up a passport application form for her.'

'Is she emigrating?'

'No, she's getting married in Rome.'

'What's wrong with getting married in Dublin?' Henrietta shook her head and tut-tutted. 'Some people have notions. Speaking of getting married, don't you think it's time you did something about your situation? Most of your friends are married or getting married. You're the only one left. You need to get out there and find yourself a successful young man.'

'I'm not the only one left, as you put it, besides there are not many young men knocking on my door.' Victoria replied with a forced laugh.

'Don't be silly, of course there are.'

'I meant young men I'd be interested in. Can we talk about something else?'

'That's you, head in the sand.'

<hr/>

After the choir's annual visit to Bray's Choral Festival, Victoria and Aiden crossed the road to the esplanade. The trees in the park alongside the esplanade were tossing their heads wildly in the raging wind. On the bandstand having their photo taken were a bride and groom. Victoria and Aiden leaned against the esplanade's railings and watched the groom try to hold his bride's veil while the wind kept whipping it out of his hand. Aiden took the cap out of his pocket and put it on his head.

'Do you think you'll ever marry?' he asked.

'Ruth once told me the tarot cards said I'd never marry.'

'I don't believe in that rubbish.' Aiden continued to look at the bride and groom. 'What about us?'

'There is no us.'

'Perhaps there should be.'

Victoria frowned.

<hr/>

The large antique clock on the mantelpiece was chiming six when Victoria stormed into the living room and smashed her handbag onto the sideboard.

'What's the matter?' her mother asked and made a point of removing Victoria's bag from the French polished inlaid sideboard.

'It's Aiden. He wants us to be more than friends.'

The instant Victoria said Aiden's name she regretted it.

'More than friends! What does he want to be, your boyfriend? Oh no, he's quite unsuitable, he's out of the question.'

Victoria stared at her mother. 'Unsuitable? Mother, who do you think we are?'

'Young lady, you need to set your sights a little higher.'

'Mother, we live in a rented terraced house in the city centre and our neighbours are working men and women.'

'We only live here because I was forced to sell our lovely home in Clontarf and rent this pathetic little house on this wretched Avenue. Walking out with a tradesman is not how a daughter of mine should behave. The man's a carpenter for God's sake.'

'Yes, he is a carpenter but he happens to be the most intelligent person I know. Mother, I ask you again, who do you think we are?'

'It's not who I think we are, it's who he is. He could never provide for you in the manner you deserve. Besides I could never live with someone like that.'

Henrietta placed her hand to her chest and took several short breaths.

'Are you planning to live with me when I marry?'

'Of course I am. I don't want to end my days in this miserable little house. I need to live in a proper home.'

'Oh.'

⁕

A north wind blew the leaves off the trees, flew them from the park and deposited them like brown snow on the roofs and in the gutters of the houses of the Avenue. The net curtains in Victoria's bedroom caressed her face and she awoke with a start. She slammed the window shut and as she lay watching the darkness of the night press against her window, she thought about Aiden.

Why on earth does he want to change things between us? Everything is fine as it is, why can't he leave things as they are? We are good friends, we talk and enjoy each other. I don't think of him as boyfriend material. She took two deep breaths. *He wants to get to know me a little better but I don't know who I am. I suppose I should try to understand him a little more.* She continued to think about Aiden and then she fell into a restless sleep.

⚓

Victoria and Aiden walked in silence along the East Pier of Howth Harbour. When they reached the lighthouse tower they sat. It was late morning and below them, the last of the fishing trawlers were unloading their catch. Above them, seagulls swirled and dived into the water.

'Have you thought about what I asked?' Aiden said watching a gull glide through the air.

'Yes, I have.'

'And your answer is yes?'

'No, it's not yes, you're a hopeless romantic. Aiden, we're close, I've never been this close to anyone in my life. If we change things between us we could lose what we have.'

'We won't lose what we have. I'm not proposing marriage. All I want is to get to know you a little more.'

'What if there is nothing more to know?'

Aiden smiled, took Victoria's hand and they walked back down the pier to the train station.

⚓

During the following months, Aiden and Victoria did grow closer. He noticed small changes in her; there was a new lightness in her voice, she smiled more easily and there was a new brightness in her eyes. One evening, as they walked home from the cinema, Victoria inquired about his mother.

'My mother is well. She asks about you, she'd like to meet you.'

'I'd like to meet her,' Victoria said and linked Aiden's arm.

'Very well, how about tea next Sunday?'

⊶⊷

When Victoria joined the Sweeney's for tea, Mr Sweeney wore his best suit and tie; Aiden had even convinced his mother not to wear her apron. The table was set with the Sweeney's best crockery and silverware. Mr Sweeney was very taken with Victoria and tried his best to entertain her. Mrs Sweeney spent a lot of her time in the kitchen.

'You were a bit stand-offish,' Aiden said to his mother when he returned from walking Victoria home.

'I wasn't stand-offish. I was my usual self.'

'No, you weren't.'

Mrs Sweeney sat by the fire and Aiden sat opposite her.

'Aiden, I think the world of you and Victoria is a nice girl, a pretty girl, really beautiful. The question I have is, why is she going out with you?'

'You are the last person in the world I thought would ever say something like that.'

'That girl does not know what she wants out of life. She likes you, she said all the right things but there is something forced about her, something's not right.'

'Mother you are being silly. When you get to know her, you'll like her more.'

⊶⊷

Victoria was strolling up the Avenue humming to herself when Mrs Green called out to her from her parlour window.

'Victoria, you never talk to me anymore,' she said, settling herself for a long chat.

'I'm so busy, what with work and the choir I never seem to have time for anything. I should learn to slow down,' Victoria said and rested her hand on the window ledge. 'How are you, Mrs Green?'

'Ah sure I'm grand, you see lots of that fellow from Auburn Street?'

To Victoria own amazement, she felt herself blush. 'I...'

'I can tell you like each other by the way you smile at him and the way he looks at you.'

Victoria's face was now crimson.

'I thought you'd be the first girl on the Avenue to get married, yet even the Fitzgibbon's girl landed herself a man. What's keeping you?'

'Are you telling that young woman how to live her life, Bridget?' said Mr Green as he came into the room. 'Don't mind my wife, Victoria. Given half the chance she'd run everybody's life.'

'I'm offering the girl some advice, Derek.'

'Advice, well that's alright,' Mr Green said with a wry smile. 'Victoria, I have to give this woman her medicine so I'm going to have to close the window, so we'll say good day to you.'

'Bye, Mr and Mrs Green,' Victoria said and continued up the Avenue.

Unseasonable flooding in counties Clare, Cork and Limerick caused a rush of claims into the offices of New Ireland Assurance Company. All through the day postmen brought bundles of letters seeking information and requests for claim forms. At five o'clock, half an hour before finishing time, Mr Finch the office manager asked Victoria if she would stay an extra hour or so to help get through the day's large amount of correspondence. Victoria agreed and as they worked she asked Mr Finch why he had chosen her to stay back and not one of the more experienced assessors.

'All the other assessors are married. You are like me, unmarried, we don't have the same demands on our time. Rest assured, Victoria. I shall make a note of this in your file. It will not go unnoticed.'

Not go unnoticed? Noted in my file? I don't give a sugar what's in my file. Does he think I want to spend the rest of my life answering enquiries and filing forms? I have a life. And he and I are not alike.

As she continued working she wondered how many other people saw her as Mr Finch did.

<hr>

The following day Victoria was walking along Stephen's Green when she noticed a young couple strolling along the busy footpath. The girl was petite and dark and the man was tall and thin. The couple stopped abruptly, looked adoringly at each other and kissed.

<hr>

Aiden was not himself all day. Victoria had spent a lovely afternoon in Powerscourt with him. She knew something was wrong but she was afraid to ask. As they stood watching the gigantic waterfall, Aiden took Victoria's hands and told her he loved her. He went down on one knee and her body tensed.

'Will you marry me and make me the happiest man in Ireland?'

Victoria looked at the water cascading over the waterfall and shuddered.

'How do you know you love someone?' she asked.

'I know I love you and I don't know what I'll do if you don't marry me. I can't be happy without you.'

'You don't know that, no one knows things like that.'

'I know we have what it takes to make a marriage work.'

'I'm afraid, really afraid. My father told me when he and my mother married they were madly in love but it didn't last. What if that happens to us?'

'I am not your father and you are not your mother.'

'I need time to think about this.'

'Take all the time you need,' said a disappointed Aiden.

That night Victoria lay in her bed and thought about the young couple on Stephen's Green and how they seemed to be looking into each other's souls. She thought about what Mrs Green said about Aiden, how special he made her feel and she knew what she wanted. She sat up in bed and started to cry.

Wearing a new white floral print, sleeveless summer dress and white high heels, Victoria waited at the entrance to Stephens's Green. When she saw Aiden, her heart jumped and when he stood in front of her she threw her arms around him and kissed him properly for the first time.

'My guess is, the answer is yes,' Aiden said, holding her slender waist.

'You'll have to wait until we're in the rose garden for your answer.'

Smiling, she took his hand and led him along the edge of the artificial lake and into the rose garden. Seated on a bench, she opened her handbag, removed a small box tied with a ribbon and handed it to him.

'Open it,' she said, looking into his face.

'This is unusual.'

He undid the ribbon, opened the box and after he removed a layer of tissue paper he found three beautiful carved wooden letters YES.

'Yes, Aiden. I love you and I'd love to be your wife.' She slipped her hand around the back of his neck, pulled him close and kissed him gently on the lips.

Aiden put his hand on her waist, pulled her closer and kissed her firmly. They kissed again and again until one of the park's gardeners tipped Aiden on the shoulder and asked them to leave.

The shaded lamp on the dressing table shone its yellow light on Victoria and the letter she was writing. Henrietta clattered into the room and placed a pile of bed linen on the end of the bed.

'Mother, you should knock before you enter my room,' Victoria said, quickly putting the letter in the top drawer of her dressing table.

'Who are you writing too?'

Victoria ignored the question.

'Mother, there is something I want to talk to you about, why don't you sit?'

'Sit down? This sounds ominous.'

Henrietta settled on the bed.

'Aiden has asked me to marry him and I have accepted his proposal.'

Henrietta's eyebrows shot upwards and she fanned her face with her right hand.

'How could you possibly contemplate marriage to that young man?'

'Mother I'm close to thirty and I want to start a life of my own.'

'But why him?'

'I love him.'

'You don't love him. You will not marry him, I forbid it.'

'Mother, for once in your life, try to be happy for me. I am going to marry Aiden and that's the end of it. He's coming here to talk to you tomorrow afternoon at two, be here and be polite.'

Long strips of sunlight fell across the rug in the living room and highlighted the carpet's worn, frayed edges. Henrietta sat at the table tapping her fingers. When she heard the knock she inhaled deeply and answered the door. Aiden was wearing a new tweed suit and a silk tie. Henrietta looked at him with disdain and without saying a word flung open the door to the parlour. She pointed to an armchair by the window.

He waited until she sat in the armchair as far from the window as possible. He smiled and sat in the armchair opposite her.

She blinked and sat up straight. 'I don't know why I agreed to this meeting but say your piece and be off with you.'

'I'm here to ask for your daughter's hand in marriage.'

Henrietta looked at Aiden in the irritating way people do when they are expecting an answer to a question they haven't asked.

'I know you don't approve of me but I love your daughter and I intend to marry her.'

'Oh do you? Let me assure you young man, you will never marry my daughter.'

'I will marry your daughter and I will make her happy.'

'How could you make Victoria happy? You are a tradesman.'

'Victoria loves me and I will make her happy.'

'You have no idea what will make my daughter happy. Enough of this silliness, I have told Victoria if she persists in this madness I will not attend the wedding.'

'That is cruel.'

'Life is cruel.' Henrietta's face had the look of a chess master who had outplayed a novice opponent.

'Mrs Lyons it is important to Victoria that her family be present at her wedding. However...' Aiden paused a moment. Henrietta looked away. '...if you cannot attend your daughter's wedding, I'm sure your husband will be happy to represent your family.'

Henrietta was outraged. 'Young man, I am a widow.'

'Mrs Lyons, I have met your husband, he is very much alive.'

Henrietta's cheeks flushed and she put her hand to her breast as if she was about to have a heart attack.

Aiden continued, relentlessly. 'I do not wish to cause you any embarrassment or hurt. All I ask is you attend your daughter's wedding and nothing more.'

Henrietta pulled a handkerchief out of the sleeve and touched her eyes. 'If I do as you ask, can I rely on you not to invite my husband?'

'Yes. And one other thing. Victoria and I hope to purchase a house nearby and you will be welcome to drop by whenever you like.'

Henrietta stood, fanning herself with the handkerchief.

'Mr Sweeney, you are not the lamb I expected.'

Victoria and Aiden visited the Happy Ring House on O'Connell Street and spent an hour choosing their wedding rings. Exiting the shop Aiden suggested, for old time's sake, that they have coffee in The Palm Grove across the street.

'Should we not go somewhere a little more fancy?'

'I'd like to go the Palm Grove.' Aiden said and smiled.

After they had ordered coffee, a tall eleven-year-old girl and a blond-haired eight-year-old boy came and stood by their table. Victoria was confused, but Aiden didn't seem at all surprised.

'Is your name Victoria?' asked the young girl.

'Yes, it is. How do you know my name?'

'I'm Sally and this is my brother Tom.'

'Well, hello Sally and Tom...'

Aiden nodded to someone sitting in the rear of the café. Victoria turned and her father waved gently to her.

'You're my sister,' said Sally.

Victoria swallowed hard.

'Yes, I am and I'm pleased to meet you Sally, and you too Tom. Would you like to sit and have some ice cream with us?'

'Yes we would,' Tom said and climbed into the seat beside Aiden. 'Could I have strawberry ice cream and red jelly?'

'I think we can organise that, and what would you like Sally?' asked Aiden.

'I'll have whatever my big sister is having,' Sally replied, sat beside Victoria and took her hand.

Aiden asked his best friend David to be his best man.

David took his responsibilities seriously; he had the groom in the church thirty minutes before the appointed time, and the wedding rings safely tucked away in the pocket of his waistcoat. He had organised and paid the priest, the sacristan, the organist and he even had the money ready for the altar boys. He placed his hand on the breast pocket of his morning suit and reassured himself his best man's speech was safe. He stood next to the groom at the altar rails in St Joseph's Church and waited on the bride to arrive.

'She's late, it's ten past the hour,' Aiden whispered.

'She's only ten minutes late, you can start worrying in twenty minutes,' David said, glancing down the packed church. 'Let's sit, take the weight off our feet.'

As the two young men sat, a slight whisper rippled down the church. Twenty minutes later, Aiden was visibly anxious. David tried to keep him calm, but then Ruth hurried down the side aisle and beckoned discreetly. David stood up and slipped along the pew towards her. 'What is it, is something wrong?'

'Yes, there is.'

When he returned to Aiden, David's face was grim and his eyes apprehensive. He sat beside his friend and spoke softly.

'I don't think Victoria's coming.'

Every muscle in Aiden's body tensed.

'Ruth went around to the house and there was no one there. She looked in the parlour window and the wedding dress was lying on the couch. Mrs Green told Ruth that Victoria and her mother drove off in a taxi more than thirty minutes ago and Victoria was in ordinary clothes. What do you want to do?'

'We'll give her five more minutes,' replied Aiden.

Six minutes later, Father Hannan sent an altar boy out to ask Aiden and David to come to the vestry. A loud murmur arose in the church as they walked out onto the altar; by the time they reached the vestry it had transformed into a great din.

'I've had a telephone call from Mrs Lyons,' said Father Hannan. 'She said with much regret she and her daughter will not be attending church today.'

Aiden's head swirled, he leaned against the vestry's wood-panelled wall and steadied himself. The priest handed him a glass of water.

'Would you like me to inform the congregation?'

'Yes, I would,' he whispered, draining the water.

The congregation quietened as Father Hannan walked along the altar rails. He stopped at the open gates and the people held their breath. The priest calmly informed the congregation the wedding would not be taking place and the mystified people swarmed out of the church.

On Monday morning, Richard Lyons arrived at Fifteen Auburn Street and asked to speak to Aiden. A tired and pinched Mrs Sweeney ushered him into the parlour and a few minutes later, Aiden joined him and sat in the darkest part of the room. Richard did not comment on Aiden's drawn appearance.

'I'm not in a talkative mood. What can I do for you?'

'I'll be brief. I'd like to say how sorry I am about what happened the other day and I'd like to explain the situation to you as best I can.'

Aiden didn't respond.

'Last week I was in Dublin on business and Victoria came to me and told me she was confused and concerned. She said she loved you but she didn't feel she loved you enough to marry you. I told her she should talk to you and the two of you could work it out.'

'She said nothing to me.'

'I know. She said she couldn't face you because she knew you would convince her everything was alright. When I asked her why she had taken so long to come to this conclusion she said she wanted to do the right thing by everyone. She wanted to love you, but wanting to love you wasn't the same as loving you. Victoria asked if I would give you this letter.'

Richard reached into his pocket, removed a white envelope and placed it on the coffee table.

'I'm sorry Aiden. You're a good man.'

When the door closed behind Richard, Aiden leaned over, picked up the letter and read it.

My dearest Aiden,

This is the hardest letter I've ever written. I am so sorry for what I've done to you. You are one of the kindest, most loving people I've met and I am ashamed of the way I treated you. I know I hurt you but in my strange demented way, I believe I did the right thing.

What I learned from you is love is not a game and it's not something you can play at, but I fear that is what I was doing. I truly wanted to love you. I tried so hard I fooled myself into believing I was in love with you. Your mother knew I was deceiving myself. She never said anything but she knew. If I had continued with my charade what a sham our marriage would have been. Marriage is hard but to try it without being truly in love would have been madness. Please don't think of me as cruel or unfeeling. I do love you and always will but the love I have for you is not the love a woman should have for her husband. Perhaps I am incapable of experiencing or expressing that kind of love.

I am going to spend some time with my father and his family in Wales. Once again I am profoundly sorry for all the pain I've caused you.

With the deepest regret,

Victoria.

⚓

Two years later on the 28th May 1952, Aiden married Roisin Murphy from Cabra in the Church of the Most Precious Blood. Halfway through the wedding ceremony Victoria entered the back of the church, stood awhile and when a tear formed in her eye she left.

CHAPTER 12

THE CONFRATERNITY MAN

It was the 8th December, the Feast of the Immaculate Conception of the Blessed Virgin Mary and a Holy Day of Obligation, and Denis Williams, a daily Mass-goer, had slept it out. He hurried to get dressed, hoping to make it to St Joseph's Church before Mass had started. Pulling on his coat, he dipped his fingers in the small plastic holy water font in his hallway, blessed himself and closed the door of Number Twenty Three behind him. The morning sky was dark and the city was in the first grip of winter. A cold wind tore up the Avenue and flapped his coat as he rushed to the church. The holy water in the granite font outside the church was frozen and an out-of-breath Denis had to tap hard on the layer of ice to get to the water.

'You're just about in time, Denis,' said the stern-faced Canon Breathnach as he stepped out of the darkness of the church porch. The Canon was a tall man whose whole being exuded nervous energy. He was the Director of the Confraternity Society, the man who on Wednesday next was going to interview Dennis for membership of the Confraternity. Denis had been fretting about the forthcoming interview and that was the reason for his bad night's sleep. The Canon smiled weakly and Dennis froze like the water in the font.

Denis nodded nervously, pulled the cap off his head and entered the church.

⊨⊣⊢⊨

On Wednesday evening when Denis knocked on the door of the parish hall, it was opened by the gaunt John Kelly, the latest recruit to the Confraternity. Denis was ushered into the dimly-lit hallway and was seated beside two other applicants. He was handed a form.

'They'll call you when they're ready. These two men are before you. Fill out the form and give it to Father Hannon when you get inside,' John Kelly said, with such gravity that he might have been sharing the third secret of Fatima.

Canon Donnacha Breathnach, the parish priest of St Joseph's, was a tall, angry-faced man who controlled the confraternity with ruthless and absolute authority. The Canon knew Denis was a man of deep faith but Denis's somewhat vacant expression and genteel quietness unsettled him, and for that the Canon had twice rejected Denis's application for Confraternity membership.

'How could a man who doesn't like sport and isn't a Gaeilgeoir represent the parish?' Canon Breathnach said to the panel after Denis's second interview.

Denis Williams was a humble man. All his adult life he had wanted to be a Confraternity Man so he could help people in the parish less fortunate than himself. He was a shy person who often became flustered when he met people. He was an only child and when his parents passed away, he took over the rental of Number Twenty Three. He lived a solitary life and if it was unexciting, it was the life he desired.

He worked as a cashier in the General Post Office in O'Connell Street. Every morning he arrived at his place of work at ten to nine, hung his overcoat, hat and scarf on his designated hook and at exactly nine o'clock pulled back the curtains on hatch 19, removed the small 'Dúnta' sign and tended to his customers. At the end of each day, he replaced the wooden 'Dúnta' sign, closed the curtains on his little hatch, retrieved his hat, coat and scarf and walked home. It was an unusual day if Denis spoke more than ten words to any of his post office colleagues or to his customers. On his way home, he always stopped in Moore's grocery store and, as today was Wednesday, he bought a small sliced pan, two slices of cheese and an onion. When he had consumed his cheese and onion sandwiches, he made his way to St. Joseph's Church Parish Hall for his third Confraternity interview.

Canon Breathnach was seated at the top of the table. Father Hannon, the society's deputy director – a position the Canon made sure was powerless – sat on his left. Maurice O'Connell, the society's equally powerless chief prefect, sat at the Canon's right. At the far end of the long and highly-polished table, an empty chair awaited Denis.

'You're a persistent man,' the Canon said, eyeing Denis. 'This is your third attempt to join the Confraternity. You realise this is your final attempt.'

'I am aware of that Canon. I have done all you asked of me. I attended Mass every day and received Holy Communion. Every week I made my confession and attended Benediction. I made the Stations of the Cross weekly and every night I prayed God will keep our priests safe.'

'Yes Denis, I have seen you in the church many times,' interjected Father Hannon. 'Good man.'

Denis smiled, but the Canon didn't. The Canon ran every Confraternity meeting like a military exercise. No one was allowed to voice an opinion except him and his deputy director Father Hannon had just usurped his absolute authority.

'Father Hannon, when your input is required I will request it, until then please keep your counsel.'

Father Hannon's face went scarlet and Maurice O'Connell bowed his head.

After a gruelling interview, the Canon paused and gave a limp smile.

'Mr Williams, I have decided to admit you provisionally into the Confraternity. You will be a sub-prefect. It will give you a chance to prove yourself. There is one proviso. When the Easter raffle tickets become available you will be expected to sell at least forty books of tickets.'

'Forty books of tickets, that's an awful lot of tickets,' said Dennis.

The Canon's response was a quick, empty smile.

'If it's too much for you. I quite understand.'

'No Canon, I can sell forty books of tickets.'

The Canon walked down the table and placed two ribbons in front of Denis. 'The yellow ribbon is a sub-prefect ribbon and the red ribbon is a Sacred Heart ribbon, both ribbons must be always worn when you are engaged in Confraternity work.'

The Canon returned to his position at the top of the table, opened a ledger, ran his long fingers down the page and in one swift movement closed the ledger and ceremoniously placed a hand on top of it.

'I'm assigning you to work with Terrance Molloy. He is a good man. He will be your mentor. You will learn a lot from him. You will accompany him on his visitations and help him distribute food and clothing to those in need in the tenements of Lower Wellington Street. Words of caution, we only give charity to the deserving poor; people who believe in the One, Holy, Roman Catholic Apostolic Church. We do not give charity to people who live in sin or those who waste our charity on drink and such. Do you understand Denis?'

'I do,' he replied and wondered at the words 'deserving poor.'

Terrance Molloy stood in a pool of lamplight outside Kennedy's Pub at the top of Lower Wellington Street and waited. Terrance was a tall, scrawny man who never smiled. He had been a Confraternity Man for ten years and was trusted implicitly by the Canon. He pulled his woolly cap down over his ears, dug his hands into the pockets of his old overcoat and stomped his feet on the freezing ground. Terrance was looking up and down the street impatiently when Denis arrived.

'O'Duill is late again, if he's not careful the Canon will get rid of him,' Terrance said to Denis. 'Steer clear of O'Duill.'

'Why is that?' asked Denis.

'The only reason the Canon has O'Duill in the Confraternity is because he owns a push-cart and brings the parcels from the parish hall for us to distribute.'

A few minutes later the grinding of iron-rimmed wheels on the cobblestones announced the arrival of Sean O'Duill. Pushing his cart in front of him, the jolly-faced, enormous man in a weather-beaten raincoat and hat, stopped beside the two Confraternity men.

'How is happy-face Molloy this fine and beautiful evening?' asked the enormous O'Duill, his soft Derry accent rising on his last word. He pulled back the canvas covering and revealed a collection of large wicker baskets. Each basket was filled with a number of parcels wrapped in brown paper.

'We'll have none of your guff, O'Duill. What kept you?'

'Terrance, my good man, I stopped to have a cup of tea with none other than himself, Archbishop John Charles McQuaid, the man in the red slippers. You know I can't refuse that man anything.'

'Oh shut up, O'Duill.'

Terrance rummaged about the baskets until he found the ones with his name pinned to the wicker lids. He handed one to Denis and held on to a second one. 'Off you go, O'Duill, the others are waiting for you,' he said as he marched away down the street.

'What kind of food is in the parcels?' asked Denis, following him.

'Flour, porridge, salt, tins of this and that, and sometimes there's a bit of fruit or vegetables.'

'Who decides who gets what?'

'The Canon decides, he has pinned a name to each parcel and we must give the parcel to that family. If a family's name is not on a parcel, they get nothing. Because it's Tuesday I've only two baskets of parcels to distribute, on Fridays I'll have six or more. You have to watch yourself around here, given half a chance the people would rob the sight from your eye. Hold on tightly to the basket and don't let anyone near it, especially the kids, they're the worst.'

Denis tightened his grip on the wicker basket. Terrance Molloy stopped at tenement house Number Fifty and pushed open the main front door. Inside the hall he pulled a candle and candleholder from his pocket and with a flick of his nicotined-stained thumbnail a match burst into flames and revealed a dark, gloomy, pungent-smelling hallway. He lit the candle, knocked on two doors on the ground floor and delivered a parcel to each family. On the second floor he delivered to three flats. When they arrived on the third-floor landing, a door opened and a pasty-faced boy peered out.

'Hey mister, you got anything for us?' The boy was about to say something else when a ferocious coughing wracked his small body.

Denis looked to Terrance who shook his head tersely.

'I don't think your family is on the list,' Denis said to the child.

'And why is that?' asked the boy's mother jutting her head out of the doorway. 'Are we not good enough for your charity? Ah, Darragh, you're wasting your breath asking them for help. They don't give to the likes of us.'

'We don't decide who gets a parcel,' interjected Terrance. 'And well you know why you're not getting anything.'

'Oh yes, the good Canon says so. Ah well then, that's alright.'

'There is no need for sarcasm. The Canon does his best, he helps a lot of deserving people.'

'Deserving people, am I not deserving? If you think that gobshite Canon is doing his best, you better think again. Come on Darragh there's a bit of porridge left after breakfast that will have to be your dinner,' the woman said and closed the door.

'That woman is a disgrace,' Terrance said as he climbed the stairs to the fourth landing.

'Why don't we have a parcel for her and her son? They look like they need help.'

'Mrs Kenny, as she calls herself, never goes to church and has far too much to say for herself. You heard what she said about the Canon. Have no dealings with her.'

Terrance knocked on the door of flat 4F and, after a minute or so, an old woman with a black shawl draped around her shoulders pulled open the door. Terrance handed the woman the last parcel in his basket.

'Thanks very much, you wouldn't have a bit of coal, would you? It's freezing in the flat.'

'We'll have some coal on Friday, Mrs Daly. I'll make sure you get some.'

'That would be lovely, thanks and good night now, you're two good men.' She closed the door.

'Now see the difference, Denis. Mrs Daly is a good decent woman, not like that old rip Kenny. We'll go to Number Fifty Three now and distribute your basket.'

After they distributed the parcels in Denis's basket, Terrance stretched and yawned. 'That's it for the night. I'm in a bit of a hurry, my mother-in-law is visiting. Would you be so good as to return the baskets to the parish hall?'

'Certainly,' Denis replied and Terrance rushed off down the stairs leaving him in the dark.

It took a minute for Denis's eyes to adjust to the blackness. As he made his way down the tenement stairs he felt something moving in the bottom of one of the baskets. He stopped. His hand patted the bottom of the basket and when his hand touched something soft he quickly withdrew it. He rushed down the stairs and as he exited the building the thing in the basket moved again. Under a streetlamp, he put his hand into the basket and grabbed the object. It was an orange. He returned to Number Fifty, walked up the stairs and knocked on the door of Mrs Kenny's flat. When the woman opened the door he handed her the orange.

'I know it's not much, but it's all I have,' he said, tipping his hat.

From nowhere the boy's hand shot out and grabbed the orange; without saying a word the boy melted back into the flat.

'Thanks for the orange. I didn't mean what I said earlier. I get so tired and fed up,' Mrs Kenny said, and with a nod, she closed the door.

That night Denis had the best night sleep he'd had in months.

Twice a week for the next two months, Denis accompanied Terrance Molloy on his visitations. On Monday nights he helped prepare the food parcels and the second-hand clothes parcels. His other duties included making sure the shrines around the church were polished and well-stocked with small white candles. He swept the church and on all major church holidays he helped members of the congregation find seats for the ceremonies.

One day, as Denis was walking down Lower Wellington Street, Mrs Kenny waved to him and scurried across the street to him. Wearing a tired yellow blouse, a long black skirt and an all-enveloping black shawl, the pale-faced woman asked Denis if she could have a word.

'I don't like to bother you but I was wondering if there was any chance you could get some clothes for my son's Holy Communion.'

'Oh, I thought you didn't go to Mass.' Denis said.

'Who told you that? Never mind, it doesn't matter. My son, like every other child, wants to look well when he makes his Communion. Do you think you could get some clothes for the boy?'

'Mrs Kenny, I don't decide who gets clothes, the Canon does.'

'Oh, I thought you might have been able to do something for me, sorry if I bothered you,' Mrs Kenny said, and with shoulders slouched she walked back across the street.

Denis was still thinking about Mrs Kenny when Mrs Daly tapped him on the arm.

'That poor woman, God love her, she's her own worst enemy. A few years ago she criticised the Canon a bit too much and he read her from the pulpit. He told her she was not welcome in his church, and the poor old devil hasn't been to St Joseph's since. I've seen her many a time at Mass in St Saviours, in Dominic Street. Her little boy is sick. I'd say it's the TB.' Mrs Daly adjusted her shawl around her shoulders. 'God must really love the poor.'

'Why is that, Mrs Daly?'

'He must love us, he made so many of us.'

⟞⟝⟞

Terrance Molloy placed a large sack of second-hand clothes on the table in front of Denis and ripped it open.

'There are four types of clothes, boys, girls, men's and women's. Make four piles and then give me a call,' Terrance said and walked away.

Denis had just finished sorting the clothes into four stacks when Terrance arrived with a second sack.

'I was wondering if we could give Mrs Kenny some clothes for her son's Holy Communion.'

Terrance looked at Denis as if he was an imbecile. 'If you did, the Canon would make sure your life wasn't worth living.'

'Her boy is sick and the woman has little or no income, they need help.'

'Who needs help?' asked the Canon, as he floated along the table on a cloud of self-importance.

'Mrs Kenny, of Wellington Street,' replied Denis. 'Her son is ill and has no clothes for his First Holy Communion.'

The Canon's eyes narrowed and he inhaled through his nose. 'And since when do you decide who receives the Confraternity's charity?'

'The woman has great need.'

'Then she should have thought of that before she denigrated Mother Church. She does not deserve our charity. She lives in sin and has not attended Mass in years.'

'But the boy is ill and she was told not to...'

'I don't wish to continue this conversation. That woman and her son are to be given nothing, do you understand?'

'Yes, Canon.'

'And never speak of her again to me. On a far more important matter, have you sold the forty books of raffle tickets you pledged to sell?'

'Not quite, I've still got a few books left.'

'That's where you should be spending your energy.'

Denis stood in Moore's grocery shop and watched the grocer slice his three slices of ham. In Denis's hand was a book of raffle tickets and he was summoning up the courage to ask the grocer if he would buy another ticket. Just then, Mrs Drake strode breezily into the shop.

'Hello Denis,' she chirped.

'If you knew how many tickets I've bought for that raffle you wouldn't ask me to buy another one,' Mr Moore said when he saw the tickets in Denis's hand. 'I think I bought a ticket from every child and adult in the neighbourhood.'

'Denis, are you selling raffle tickets?' asked Mrs Drake.

Denis did not know what to do, a Protestant woman enquiring about a Catholic raffle. What if she won? What would the Canon say? What would he do? Denis remembered the six unsold books of tickets sitting on the mantelpiece in his home and decided to honestly answer the woman's question.

'Yes, I am. The tickets are two pence each or a book of seven is a shilling. They are for the *parish* raffle,' Denis said hoping his emphasis on the word 'parish' would signal there was no need for her to buy a ticket.

'It doesn't matter if it's a parish raffle as long as it's for charity,' Mrs Drake said and handed Denis a shilling. 'As the Very Reverend Henry Boyle says, we are all God's children.'

'Oh yes,' replied Denis as he reluctantly accepted the protestant's woman's shilling.

Rain bounced off the footpath and up the back of Denis's trousers as he waited on the dour-faced Terrance Molloy and the jolly Sean O'Duill with his cart to arrive.

'Shocking night,' said O'Duill, as he shook the rain off the top of his hat.

'That it is,' Denis replied and searched the cart for baskets with Terrance's name pinned to them.

A loud cough announced the arrival of Terrance Molloy. He pushed Denis aside, rummaged through the cart and quickly found four baskets with his name pinned to them. With each man carrying two baskets, they made their way down the street. When they arrived at Number Fifty, Terrance pushed open the door, lit his candle and entered the building.

Making their deliveries the two men worked their way up the stairs. Terrance was a little ahead of Denis and had finished talking to Mrs Daly on the fourth floor when he looked over the banisters and saw Denis tap quietly on Mrs Kenny's door. A tired-looking Mrs Kenny pulled open the door and when she saw Denis, she half-smiled. Denis heard a noise on the landing above and looked up. When he was certain he was not being observed, he removed a parcel from under his coat and handed it to Mrs Kenny.

'It's a few clothes for Darragh. I hope they fit. Don't tell anyone where you got them,' Denis said, and looked around again. He removed a small Confraternity envelope from his inside pocket and handed it to the woman. 'And here's a few shillings to buy whatever else you need.'

Tears of astonishment and joy glistened in the woman's eyes. Denis indicated she should go inside.

'The blessings of God on you,' she whispered as she closed the door.

'Were you talking to that Kenny woman?' Terrance asked sharply when Denis joined him on the fourth-floor landing.

'Yes, I said hello to her. How is Mrs Daly?'

'Oh she's grand,' Terrance said and looked at Denis from under his heavy eyelids.

The last rays of the spring's evening sun were dancing on the water of the Basin as the gaunt John Kelly and Terrance Molloy walked to the last Confraternity meeting before Easter.

'I don't think you're right there,' John Kelly said, scratching his head. 'Denis wouldn't do anything like that, he's an honest man.'

'I saw him slip the parcel to the woman. He thought I didn't notice but I did. I don't miss much. I have to inform the Canon.'

Once in the parish hall, Terrance Molloy went straight to the Canon's office. As he listened, the Canon's eyes bulged, dark veins stood out on his forehead and his nostrils flared.

'Are you sure what you are telling me is true?'

'I saw it with my own eyes, Canon.'

'Thank you, Terrance, you were right to bring the matter to my attention, you did your duty. There was always something about Williams I didn't like.'

The parish hall was a busy place that night. Maurice O'Connell, the Confraternity treasurer, was making the final entries into the ledgers, two men were putting raffle tickets stubs into the drum and Father Hannon was welcoming other members as they arrived for the meeting. Canon Breathnach sat in his office finalising the talk he was about to give the men. Ten minutes before the meeting was to begin, Father Hannon gathered up the ledgers, went to the Canon's office and presented them to him.

'They seem to be in order,' the young priest said placing the ledgers on the Canon's desk.

'Has Denis Williams arrived yet?'

'Yes, he arrived a few minutes ago, Canon.'

'I know you think I'm hard on the men,' the Canon said after signing the book and screwing the top back on his silver fountain pen.

'Not so Canon, you have much more experience of these matters than I do. I trust your judgement. May I ask why you appoint prefects for only one year at a time? Would five years not be a better time span?'

'Appointing them for one year at a time is a wonderfully effective way of keeping the men in line. It keeps them alert and attentive to their duties. If they become careless they know I will shame them and replace them. For instance Denis Williams, I intend to make an example of him tonight, this will be his last night as a Confraternity Man.'

'But he seems such a harmless fellow?'

'He certainly is not a harmless fellow, the man is a troublemaker. Father Hannon, I want you to chair the meeting this evening.'

'Oh,' replied a surprised Father Hannon. 'It will be my privilege.'

'Before the raffle begins, I want you to call on me to make a special announcement. And there's one other thing ...'

<hr>

Every seat around the long table was taken. Denis sat opposite his mentor Terrance Molloy. Father Hannon sat at the top of the table. Everything was progressing well, or as well as any parish meeting could, when Father Hannon announced that Canon Breathnach wanted to make an important pronouncement.

The Canon stood, pulled himself to his full height and looked around the meeting hall. He removed the biretta from his head and ran a hand dramatically through his thick hair. A few of the men bowed their heads, hoping it was not them that were about the feel the lash of the Canon's tongue. Clearly thinking he was a great barrister in a major criminal trial, or perhaps even the great Liberator Daniel O'Connell himself addressing parliament, the Canon began.

'Before we proceed any further I would like to draw your attention to a man who pretends to be a good Confraternity Man but is a man who knowingly pays scant regard to our values and principles. A man who thinks he is even above the law of the land, but more importantly, he thinks he is above the laws of Mother Church. I am talking about a man who has stolen goods and money from the Confraternity, a man who has taken it upon himself to decide who should receive Confraternity's goods and monies, a man who has the gall to sit at the table with you good men. I am talking about the hypocrite, the liar and the thief, Denis Williams.'

Some of the men gasped, others shook their heads in disbelief, while a few demanded Denis's immediate ejection from the meeting. Struck dumb, Denis looked at the Canon in dismay.

'Quiet, please,' said Father Hannon, then continued as he and the Canon had agreed earlier. 'Canon Breathnach, would you please clarify and expand on what you have said? What you are accusing Mr Williams of is very serious.'

'Yes it is serious, extremely serious, and I do not make my claims lightly. I have an eyewitness to the event.' Once again the meeting burst into murmurings and when the men quietened the Canon continued, 'Terrance Molloy, tell us what you witnessed on Friday night, two weeks ago.'

Terrance stood and, avoiding Denis's eyes, spoke. 'On Friday night, two weeks ago, I looked over the banisters of 50 Lower Wellington Street and saw Denis Williams knock on Mrs Kenny's flat and hand the woman a brown paper parcel.'

'And what was in the parcel?'

'Confraternity clothes.'

'Is Mrs Kenny someone who regularly receives parcels Confraternity charity?'

'No Canon, we never give Mrs Kenny anything.'

'Mr Denis Williams you have been accused of misappropriating Confraternity clothes and giving them to Mrs Kenny,' said a grave-faced Father Hannon. 'What have you to say for yourself?'

All eyes focused on Denis. The Canon returned to the top of the table and resumed his seat. Denis rose and looked at the Canon, shaking his head.

'Goodness gracious, is that what you think of me? I can assure you Canon I stole or misappropriated nothing.'

Father Hannon repositioned his biretta on his head and glanced at the Canon, who gave an almost imperceptible nod. 'Very well then, Mr Williams. Tell us, in your own words, what happened.'

'Well, I was telling Mr Moore, my greengrocer, about Darragh, Mrs Kenny's son and his lack of clothes for his Holy Communion when Mrs Drake, the protestant woman who lives on the Avenue, overheard me. The good woman said her son had grown out of some of his clothes and she would be happy to give them to Darragh. I said that would be lovely, so Mrs Drake parcelled up her son's old suit, shirt and a pullover, and that is what Terrance Molloy saw me give Mrs Kenny.'

The Canon's eyes bulged more than usual and he jumped to his feet. 'A likely story. Terrance, tell the meeting the rest of what you witnessed?'

'I saw Denis Williams hand Mrs Kenny a small brown Confraternity envelope filled with Confraternity money.'

'Thank you, Terrance.'

Denis looked across the table at Maurice O'Connell, the Confraternity's treasurer. 'Mr O'Connell, have I access to Confraternity monies?'

'No,' the treasure replied. 'You are on probation, only full prefects have access to Confraternity money.'

'Mr O'Connell, in your financial report earlier you stated that the books balanced?'

'I did and they do balance, all monies are accounted for, not a penny is missing.'

'Thank you.' Denis's eyes returned to the Canon. 'Canon, if I have no access to Confraternity monies and the books balance, what money are you accusing me of stealing?'

'I don't know how you did it but you were seen giving Confraternity money to Mrs Kenny,' the Canon said and pounded the table with his fist.

'That is not so,' Denis said softly.

'Are you saying Mr Molloy is telling lies?' asked Father Hannon.

'No, Mr Molloy is telling you what he saw.'

The men around the table had a collective intake of breath.

'So I am right, you are a thief,' interjected the Canon.

'Not so, Canon. I wanted Mrs Kenny to believe the Confraternity gave her money, so I put five shillings of my own money in an old, discarded, Confraternity envelope and gave it to her.'

A great murmur fanned around the table.

'That seems to me to be an honest explanation of what happened,' interjected the jolly Sean O'Duill. 'Canon Breathnach, do you have anything more to say to Denis?'

In the silence that followed the Canon's face glowed so red some of the men became concerned for him. 'Perhaps I was a bit hasty in drawing my conclusions,' he blustered, squirming in his seat. 'If I was wrong, I apologise.'

'I accept your apology,' Denis replied and the Canon glared at him.

'Let's get to the raffle,' Father Hannon said, delighted to be able to change the conversation.

Maurice O'Connell wheeled the wooden raffle drum filled with tickets stubs into the room. He flipped open the tiny trap door and the gaunt John Kelly's hand withdrew three tickets. The third prize of a box of chocolates was won by George Brust, of Blessington St, the second prize of a bottle of whiskey, was won by Joe Brennan of Geraldine Street, and the first prize of two geese was a ticket sold by Denis.

'Read out the winner's name, Maurice,' said Father Hannon.

'Mrs Drake, of the Avenue,' said Maurice.

A stunned silence fell on the meeting.

'Isn't she a protestant?' asked Terrance Molloy.

'Yes she is,' replied Denis.

'Canon Breathnach, will you as per usual visit the prize winners and personally present them with their prizes?' asked Sean O'Duill.

'What?' All eyes turned to the Canon. 'I...I...I suppose so,' replied the Canon, his eyes almost bulged out of their sockets.

Unable to contain himself any longer the Canon rose, walked out of the meeting and slammed his office door behind him. Denis stood, removed the two Confraternity ribbons from his jacket and placed them on the table.

'There is one other matter I would like to address. I would like to inform the meeting that as of tonight I no longer wish to be a member of the Confraternity. Goodnight.' He put on his coat, scarf and cap and left.

The following day a mortified Canon Breathnach called to Mrs Drake's home and presented her with her prize of the two geese. A surprised but delighted Mrs Drake graciously accepted the prize and, after a moment's thought, spoke.

'Canon, I hope you don't think me impertinent, but Denis Williams told me about Mrs Kenny and her poor sick boy, would you be a dear and give one of the geese to the woman?' A flabbergasted Canon almost gasped. 'She is one of your parishioners, isn't she?'

'Yes, she is.'

'I think it would be a nice thing to do, don't you. I believe the woman lives in Lower Wellington Street.'

'I know where the woman lives.' The Canon calmed himself. 'I'll drop it into her on my way back to St Joseph's.'

'Very good, and happy Easter to you Reverend, sorry Father. I'm all of a dither. I never won anything in my life before, this is simply wonderful.'

Mrs Drake was still talking when she closed the door.

CHAPTER 13

LAURA'S LIFE

Laura O'Connor – or Miss O'Connor, as she liked to call herself – was a religious person and a daily communicant who went to confession every week in St Joseph's Church. She felt there was something magical about going to confession. Walking into the semi-dark, near-empty church always made her feel she was visiting God in his home. On the 3rd March 1950, she knelt in the pew near Father Hannon's confessional box and when the last person had exited, she entered the silent, shadowy box. She was admiring the small crucifix above the hatch when the little wooden door slid back to reveal the silhouette of Father Hannon's bowed head.

'Make your confession,' the priest said in that distant solemn voice, priests often affect.

When Laura explained that she had no sins to confess, the puzzled priest turned his head to her.

'Why have you come to confession?'

'Because I like to be near God,' answered Laura. 'And I would like you to tell me the story of the "Miracle of The Loaves and Fishes".'

Father Hannon's hand went to his head; he remembered Father Keogh telling him of a woman who came to him in confession and asked to be told the story of "The Marriage of Cana". He placed his hands on his knees and told Laura the New Testament story.

⟞⊹⊹⟝

In times of stress Laura talked to herself and, more upsetting for those that witnessed it, she answered herself. Laura lived in Number Seventeen on the Avenue and loved her home so much she had not changed a thing in it since her mother's death, three months ago.

It was her home, it was lovely and why-o-why would she change a single thing? It was simply perfect. Laura was a neat person, some would say fastidious, even pernickety. She washed the living room and kitchen floor every Friday and meticulously cleaned the gas cooker after every meal. On the top of the chest of drawers in her bedroom was a lace doily on which stood a small Child of Prague statue. In front of the statue in a little red box was Laura's most cherished procession, her silver-plated Miraculous Medal and chain.

Laura rose every morning at the same time and had tea and two slices of Boland's bread for breakfast. Once, when the grocer, Mr Moore, didn't have a Boland's turnover and offered her a Kennedy's turnover, she got very upset.

'You know I don't eat Kennedy's bread and never offer it to me again,' she had told him.

Half an hour later, Laura returned to the shop and apologised sincerely to Mr Moore.

Most of the time Laura was a happy person, but today she was anxious. She had a second appointment with Mr Regan, a specialist in what she described as 'lumps and bumps'. Mr Regan was a tall, thin man; he had a mop of thick, black hair with only a whisper of grey. He was a serious, severe-looking person who never indulged in small talk or in light conversation.

After he'd greeted Laura he sat behind his desk, opened her file and, with his eyes on the page, read his diagnosis aloud to her. His words floated around the room and only a few dropped into her brain. When the doctor finished speaking, he wrote a prescription and said slowly to her.

'The first pills are sleeping pills, they will help you get a good night's rest. The second pill will dull the pain from the lumps under your arms; the pills will also help reduce the swelling. If all goes well, in a month or so we can operate. Do you have any questions?'

Laura shook her head and thanked the doctor. When the door closed behind her, Mr Regan knew why he sometimes hated his job. It had been two years since he'd last seen Laura and she had not attended any of her post-operation appointments.

Laura took the bus to St Mary's Nursing Home in Rathmines to visit her late mother's eighty-year-old friend, Emma Martin. As the bus crossed the city, Laura tried to remember exactly what the doctor had said to her. She remembered him saying it was urgent and he had used that word she didn't understand, or want to understand.

'A mastectomy,' she said out loud and the man sitting beside her glanced disapprovingly at her. When Laura repeated the word again a large woman in a black shawl put her arm around her child and glared ferociously at her.

Ignoring her fellow passengers, Laura decided to think about Emma. She liked visiting Emma because Emma was always so happy to see her. The two women laughed and talked and their time together passed so quickly that when the nurse told Laura visiting time was over, it was as ever a surprise.

Later, when the bus brought her home to Berkeley Road, Laura went into Dargan's Chemist and had her prescription filled.

Sitting by the fire at home, she tried to remember more of what Mr Regan had said. A knock on the front door interrupted her thoughts. It was Mrs Emmet, her immediate neighbour; she wanted Laura to come and look after her baby while she and her husband went to confession. Laura was delighted to oblige and agreed without hesitation; she got her coat and followed Mrs Emmet next door.

Mr Emmet, a small-eyed man with a red beard and a scarcity of hair on his head, opened the door and grunted a wordless greeting to Laura. Laura often wondered why a refined young woman like Mrs Emmet could be attracted to such a rough-looking man but she said nothing; as her mother said, 'there's no accounting for taste'.

When Mrs Emmet told Laura that baby Finn was asleep, Laura was disappointed; she so wanted to play with the tiny boy. Putting on a brave face she smiled and told the Emmets they should take their time, there was no need to rush home. Mr and Mrs Emmet left for church and Laura went upstairs to check on the sleeping Finn.

Standing over the baby she remembered her visits two years ago to Mr Regan and what he said to her before he performed the hysterectomy. *'You do know after the operation you will not be able to have children.'*

Laura leaned over the cot and as she touched the baby's tiny hand, tears formed in her eyes. She went downstairs, made a pot of tea and sitting by the fire tried again to remember more of what Mr Regan had said to her.

'A double mastectomy,' that's what he had said. *'If the operation is successful, and it's a big if, it will take time, a long time, to fully recover.'*

'I don't want to think about that,' Laura said out loud. She was still trying not to think about it when a key turned in the front door. She looked at her watch; an hour had passed.

'Will you have a cup of tea with us?' Mrs Emmet asked when she took off her coat.

'No thank you. I'd better be off, I have so much to do at home,' Laura replied.

Mr Emmet closed the hall door behind Laura. 'That woman is an odd sort of person, harmless, I suppose, but next time we should ask your sister to look after the baby,' he said. 'Leaving Finn with someone like her gives me the creeps.'

Standing outside the Emmets' house searching in her handbag for her keys, Laura heard every word Mr Emmet said.

On Saturday morning Laura rose early, determined to make the most of the day. She washed, picked out the new white blouse and blue skirt she had bought in Pims, brushed her hair, opened the little red box on the top of her dresser and placed the silver-plated Miraculous Medal and chain around her neck. She admired herself in the wardrobe mirror and was pleased with what she saw. After breakfast, she walked through the Blessington Basin and took a number 19 bus to Glasnevin Cemetery.

Laura was not a regular visitor to the cemetery. When she wanted to talk to her mother all she had to do was think about her and talk. But today she wanted to be as close as she possibly could be to the only person who ever truly loved her for herself. Laura adored her mother, she loved the way her mother talked to her, held her hand, the way she advised her and even the way her mother smelt. Three months ago, when her mother passed away, Laura had been heartbroken and inconsolable. She had tried hard to forgive God for taking her mother but she couldn't. Now she suspected it was because she still hadn't properly forgiven Him, that He had visited the same illness on her. After all, she'd been doing just fine ignoring Mr Regan for the last two years, yet suddenly her mother's sickness was coming to get her. Laura arranged the flowers on her mother's grave and continued to tell her mother her thoughts about God. Mother agreed God is not always fair but God is God and sometimes he isn't nice. Mid-conversation she noticed an older couple staring at her with 'that look' on their faces. Laura smiled at them and the couple hurried off. She remained at the graveside until a nearby church bell tolled one o'clock, then she said goodbye to her mother and left.

A happier Laura took the bus into town and went to her favourite restaurant, the Red Rooster in Abbey Street, for lunch. She loved the restaurant, it was so inviting with its rows of tables each with a tartan tablecloth and a pretty vase of fresh flowers. She loved the comfortable red leather seats and the colourful paintings on the walls. She loved the warm, sweet smell of baking that flowed from the restaurant's kitchen; yes, everything in the Red Rooster was just lovely.

Roast chicken and ham, roast potatoes, peas and gravy is what Laura ordered from the abrupt young waitress. When her steaming hot meal arrived Laura leaned over the plate of food, inhaled the beautiful aromas and said, 'This is lovely, I'm going to enjoy this.'

The stony-faced waitress stared at Laura and then hurried away.

Nearly three years before her mother's death, they had been having lunch in The Red Rooster when a tall, freckled-faced, red-headed young man and his mother sat at the table beside them. Laura was stealing a glimpse at the young man when she accidentally knocked a knife off the table. The freckled-faced young man quickly retrieved the knife and as he handed it to Laura their hands touched and her heart pumped so hard she blushed. Then when the young man smiled at her she felt all giddy and girly. Laura's mother started to chat with the young man's mother and soon all four were chatting and talking like old friends. The woman introduced herself as Mrs Louise Higgins and her son as Liam Higgins.

The following month when she and her mother arrived at the Red Rooster, to Laura's delight Liam and his mother were sitting at the large table near the window. Mrs Higgins invited Laura and her mother to join them. Mrs O'Connor deliberately sat beside Mrs Higgins so Laura could sit beside Liam. At first, the young people were a little shy with each other but after a few minutes they were chatting away like old friends. Mrs Higgins kept a close eye on her son; she decided on what he would have to eat and when it came time for dessert, she ordered for him. Laura thought, *that's a little peculiar!* But as her mother often said 'people can be strange'.

For the next four months, on the first Wednesday of the month, the two families met and Laura and Liam's feelings for each other grew. On their fifth meeting, Liam asked Laura if she would like to go with him to the National Gallery to see *The Marriage of Strongbow and Aoife* painting. Mrs Higgins said softly, 'We have not discussed this, Liam.'

'We don't have to discuss everything, Mother. I would like to take Laura to see the painting. Laura, would you like to go with me to see the painting?'

Laura looked at Mrs Higgins and then at her mother and when Mother nodded ever so slightly, Laura said she would love to see the painting. After further discussion, the two young people arranged to meet in the foyer of the National Gallery at two in the afternoon on the following Friday. For Laura, Friday was a long time coming. On the day of the visit, she changed her clothes at least five times. Each time her mother assured her she looked beautiful and each time Laura said, 'Not beautiful enough for Liam.'

A five to two, she was waiting in the foyer.

At two o'clock sharp, a car stopped outside the gallery and a suited Liam stepped out. When Laura saw him her heart danced, and when he saw Laura he wanted to run to her. But he remembered what his father had said to him, about taking his time, so he walked slowly to her and then said 'Hello' before escorting her to the painting.

Laura thought *The Marriage of Strongbow and Aoife* was the most beautiful, most wonderful painting she had ever seen. Standing in front of the enormous work of art, Liam took Laura's hand and she was so happy she nearly cried. Afterwards, they went to the Mount Claire Hotel for tea and cake. While they were having their tea Liam removed a small red leather box from his pocket and placed it on the table in front of her.

'That's for you,' he said and his freckled face flushed.

Laura opened the little box and her face beamed with delight. In the box was the most beautiful shiny Miraculous Medal and chain she had ever seen. He explained the medal once belonged to his grandmother and he would like Laura to have it. He was placing the medal around her neck when a man approached and introduced himself as Liam's father. Liam's eyes went dark and he frowned. Mr Higgins said hello to Laura and was asking her how she liked the painting when Liam spoke very loudly.

'I don't want to go home yet, it's too early.'

'Liam you know what we agreed, say goodbye to your friend, Laura,' Mr Higgins said ever so gently.

'Goodbye Laura,' Liam said and stormed out of the hotel lounge.

Laura was sad Liam was unhappy, she wanted to go after him and talk to him and thank him for the lovely present but Mr Higgins said Liam was upset and needed some quiet time.

Liam and Laura and their mothers continued to meet every first Wednesday and each following Friday Laura and Liam arranged to visit a museum or go to a park. One Friday Liam took Laura to the cinema and afterwards she took him to Clerys and bought him a pair of leather gloves.

'Watch, this is the exciting part,' Laura said after she handed the sales assistant some money.

The sales assistant wrote an invoice slip and placed the invoice and the money into a small cylinder. She placed the cylinder into a machine that had a network of long tubes, wires and cords attached to it. The sales assistant pulled on a cord. With a sucking sound, the cylinder shot upwards inside the tube and travelled overhead along the wires to a cash office somewhere high in the building. A few minutes later the cylinder clunked back. The sales lady removed the contents of the returned cylinder and handed Laura her receipt and her change.

'That was exciting,' said Liam. 'Will we buy something else and watch it again?'

'No, I have no more money,' said Laura, and they left the store.

The following Wednesday when Laura suggested they visit Fossett's Circus, Mrs Higgins shook her head.

'Liam doesn't like circuses,' she said. 'The way the circus people treat their animals upsets him.'

'I would like to go to the circus. Mother you told me to make my own decisions, well I want to go to the circus.'

'Very well, if that's what you want, Liam,' Mrs Higgins said, with a forced smile.

On Friday at three o'clock, Laura and Liam entered the big top of Fossett's Circus and took their seats. After three jugglers and a team of tightrope walkers finished their acts, the clowns danced around the perimeter of the circus ring while circus workers constructed a huge temporary cage. When the clowns finished their act a huge red curtain within the cage was whooshed away and revealed a pride of snarling lions. The ringmaster introduced the lion tamer and a dark-skinned man carrying a whip and a chair bowed to the audience and entered the cage. The audience cheered, the lion tamer cracked his whip, shouted a command and the pride of lions paraded around the cage. The lion tamer cracked his whip again, shouted another command and the big male lion jumped onto a small circular platform in the centre of the cage and roared. The audience oohed and ahhed and applauded loudly after each trick but

Liam grew quiet; he hunched forward and placed his hands between his knees.

'He's hurting the lions,' he said and began to rock back and forward.

'He's a lion tamer, he wouldn't hurt them,' Laura tried to assure him.

'Tell him to stop, he's hurting the lions,' Liam said and started to babble incoherently.

People glanced disapprovingly at Liam but he continued to babble and rock back and forth. Then his head flew wildly from side to side and parents quickly moved their children away.

'I don't know what to do,' Laura said looking around. 'Help him, somebody help him.'

As if from nowhere Mr Higgins appeared and put his arm around his son and held him tightly. When Liam quietened down, Mr Higgins walked him and Laura to his car.

'When Liam gets frightened or over-excited, he can have a fit,' Mr Higgins explained to Laura as he drove her home. 'He'll need lots of rest but he'll be his old self in a day or two.' When they arrived at her home on the Avenue, Mr Higgins wished her well. She said goodbye to Liam and watched the car drive away down the Avenue.

The following first Wednesday of the month, Liam and his mother failed to arrive at The Red Rooster. Laura was devastated. When it happened again the following month Laura was inconsolable. She longed to see Liam but she had no address for him and no way of contacting him. Laura's mother tried to comfort her daughter but all Laura knew was Liam had disappeared from her life.

Sitting in the Red Rooster Restaurant revisiting all those memories upset Laura, so she decided to visit the place in the city that always made her happy, Stephen's Green. There was so much to see and do in the Green, she could stroll around the park's gardens, admire the seasonal flowers and shrubs and do what she liked most; she could feed the ducks and the swans. Walking along the edge of the pond she searched in her handbag for the small brown paper bag of bread she brought from home. Then she remembered, she left it on the living room table, and she stamped her foot. Fifty yards ahead a seven-year-old girl in a pink dress was throwing small chunks of bread to the ducks and swans. Laura approached the child and asked if she would like some help feeding the ducks. The girl hid the bag behind her back.

'Let me help you,' Laura said; she reached around the child and took the bag from the little girl's hand. Furious, the girl ran at Laura. Laura stepped aside and the child plunged into the pond. Pandemonium broke out, the girl's mother screamed, Laura reached out to help the child but the girl was beyond her reach. A red-faced gardener shouted at Laura and a young man jumped into the pond and lifted the terrified child to safety. The girl's mother hugged her child and shouted at Laura, 'Imbecile, you should be locked up.'

The red-faced gardener grabbed Laura by the arm and escorted her to the Fusiliers Gate.

'The world would be a better place without your kind in it, if I ever see you here again I'll call the police,' the gardener said, and he pushed a distraught Laura out of the park.

That night at home a very upset Laura sat at an unlit fire. The silence of the house wrapped itself around her like a dead thing and she nearly screamed from loneliness and pain. She fervently wished her mother or Liam was there to comfort her. She was frightened, confused and felt so alone. She hadn't taken her medicine that day and the lumps under her arms were sore to touch.

The headaches too were getting worse and sometimes she felt dizzy. She wanted the pain to stop and she wanted answers to the questions that were plaguing her. *I'm always nice to people but they're not always nice to me, why is that?* On and on the questions came and when she could take it no longer she went to bed.

Laying in the darkness of her bedroom, her thoughts continued to plague her.

Why do people act strange around me? Some people pretend they don't see me and walk right by me, why do they do that? Some of them even smirk and laugh, they think I'm stupid, but I'm not stupid. The woman in Stephen's Green should not have called me an imbecile, I am not an imbecile and why did the gardener say the world would be a better place without me? God, why did you take Mammy? That was a terrible thing to do. Mammy, I love you, you should not have left me. And Liam where are you? Are you alright? I just want to know if you are alright.

She clenched her fist and pounded on the blanket. 'Leave me alone,' she said out loud to her thoughts.

The following morning Laura rose at her usual time, had breakfast and attended Mass in St Joseph's Church. Mrs Quinn kneeling in a pew behind her overheard her say, 'God, I hope you don't mind but I so want to see my mother, I need to see her and talk to her and I have to find out what happened to Liam. Tell Mammy I won't be long.'

Laura returned home and placed a large glass of milk and the two bottles of pills Mr Regan had prescribed for her on the living room table. She went to Mammy's bedroom and found her mother's old pills. She lined the six small bottles in a neat line on the table and, one after another she swallowed every pill. She went to her bedroom, lay on her bed and holding the Miraculous Medal in one hand and a photograph of her mother in her other she fell into a deep sleep and never again woke up.

CHAPTER 14

THE FAINTING ALTAR BOY

Father Keogh was tired, very tired. He had imbibed a little too much the previous evening and he was now paying the price. He stood in the wood-panelled vestry of St Joseph's Church and swallowed the last of the fizzing Alka-Seltzer. He placed the empty glass quietly in the vestry sink and slipped an alb over his head. He was settling it around his ample body when Liam Cooney, an altar boy, strolled into the vestry.

Father Keogh closed his eyes. 'Liam, what are you doing here?'

'I'm the Mass server, father.'

'No you're not. Tom Brady and Don Mooney are rostered for this Mass.'

The priest kissed the Mass stole and placed it solemnly around his neck.

'Father, Tom Brady and his family went on their holidays to the Silver Strand and Tom asked me to do the Mass for him. Do you know the Silver Strand?'

'Of course I know Silver Strand, that's beside the point. Liam, I don't want to be pedantic but you don't *do* the Mass, you *serve* the Mass.'

The altar boy nodded as if he understood the difference.

'What about young Mooney, where is he?'

'He's sick, father.'

'Then who is serving the Mass with you?'

'No one, Father. I'm on my own.'

'You know this is a nuptial Mass?'

'A what?'

'A nuptial Mass, a wedding Mass.' Father Keogh exhaled deeply.

'Oh, who's getting married?'

'It doesn't matter whose getting married. I'm asking you, do you know how to serve a nuptial Mass?'

'Yes, Father.' The priest relaxed. 'Tom told me what to do.'

The priest glared at the boy.

'Told you what to do? So you never actually served a nuptial Mass?'

'No, Father.'

'Good God,' the priest said and gracefully swung the chasuble over his alb. Then he remembered the main problem about Liam. 'If I remember correctly, you've fainted twice on me, haven't you?'

'Yes, and once on Fr Hannan. And once on a missionary priest.'

'Have you ever managed to get through a Mass without fainting?'

'Oh yes, Father, lots.'

'You're not going to faint on me during this Mass are you, Liam?'

'Oh no, Father, I only faint when I get upset.'

'Then we'll have to make sure we don't upset you,' the priest muttered to himself.

'What, Father?'

'Nothing.'

The clock in the vestry struck the hour, the organist started to extemporise and the old rotund priest looked out the cruciform window in the vestry door.

'Everybody's here, the groom is at the altar, we'd better begin.'

The altar boy positioned himself in front of the vestry door. Father Keogh reached for the door's brass handle, then stopped.

'Liam, where is the holy water bucket and the aspergillum?'

'The what, Father?'

'The holy water bucket and sprinkler?'

Liam dashed out of the vestry and returned with the bucket and aspergillum. The priest went to open the door again, then stopped abruptly.

'Where did you get the water in the bucket?'

'From the tap, Father,' Liam said after a suspiciously long pause.

'The holy water tap is in a locked cabinet and you don't have the key.' The old priest stood tall. 'Did you put regular tap water in the holy water bucket?'

The boy looked down and his eyes darted left and right.

Without saying a word the incensed priest moved his chasuble to one side, lifted his alb, rummaged in his trouser pocket and handed the boy his set of keys.

'Go and fill the bucket with holy water and be quick about it.'

When Liam returned, Father Keogh opened the door and the altar boy, followed by the priest walked out of the vestry. Liam knelt on the high altar's lower step. The priest stopped in front of the altar gates, nodded at the groom and waited for the bride and her father to walk down the aisle.

Then he cleared his throat loudly.

Liam looked around and saw the priest glaring at him. He suddenly remembered his first duty was to open the gates. He jumped to his feet, rushed in front of the priest and tripped over the kneelers. Just as the bride and her father reached the top of the aisle, he threw open the gates.

For the next short while, the ceremony went without a hitch. When it came time to bless the young couple, Father Keogh turned to the altar boy and muttered under his breath, 'Where's the holy water bucket and aspergillum?'

'They're on the altar table, Father.'

'Would you be so kind as to get them?' said the priest, a little louder than he'd intended.

The bride looked questioningly at Father Keogh and in response he shook his head apologetically.

Liam hurried to the altar table, grabbed the holy water bucket and sprinkler and rushed back to the bride and groom. Father Keogh said a few more prayers, took the aspergillum out of the water bucket and was about to sprinkle the kneeling couple with holy water when a dog barked in the back of the church. The congregation turned to look. Father Keogh decided to return the sprinkler to the bucket. Distracted by the dog, Liam took a step aside and the aspergillum clattered to the tiled floor.

'Pick it up,' said the priest sharply.

The best man assumed Father Keogh was talking to him and when he bent down to get the sprinkler so did Liam; their heads collided with a thud. The boy dropped the bucket and with a crash and a whoosh; the bucket and sprinkler bounced off the floor and water flooded around the bride. With a scream, the bride jumped to her feet, holding up her dress.

'Jesus,' the best man exclaimed, then slapped his hand over his mouth.

'Are you alright?' the bride asked Liam as she helped him to his feet.

'I'm alright,' he replied, a little dazed. 'But the holy water bucket is empty.'

'Liam, give me the bucket and go to the altar and sit on the server's seat!' Then, turning to the best man, Father Keogh asked, 'Are you hurt?''

'Just continue with the ceremony, please,' groaned the best man, touching his bruised forehead.

The service continued without incident until the exchanging of rings. Father Keogh asked the best man to place the rings on the silver paten. When the puzzled best man asked the priest where the paten was, the priest whispered, 'In the altar boy's hand.'

'No, it's not,' whispered the best man in return.

'Where's the silver paten?' the priest said to Liam, ever so slowly.

'It's over there on the altar table. Should I get it, Father?'

'Yes, please do,' Father Keogh replied, barely concealing his annoyance.

When Liam returned, the best man placed the wedding rings and a silver sovereign on the paten and the altar boy held them out in front of the bride and groom. Father Keogh scowled at Liam, the boy's hand shook and the rings and the sovereign started to rattle. The groom reached out, took hold of his side of the paten and steadied it. The groom winked at Liam and Liam sighed with relief.

When it was time for the wine and water to be brought to the altar, Liam discovered the cruets were empty. He walked quickly up the side steps of the altar.

'*Pisssss!*' he hissed to the praying priest.

The astonished priest glanced to his left. 'What is it?'

'There's no wine or water in the cruets.'

'Did you not fill the cruets before Mass?'

'No, Father. Should I fill them now?'

'Yes, I think that would be a good idea.'

'Right, Father,' replied the altar boy and he marched off towards the vestry.

'Liam,' Father Keogh called after him.

The boy stopped.

'You don't have the keys to the wine cabinet.' The priest swung his chasuble to one side, lifted his alb to his waist, rummaged in the pocket, found his keys and handed them to Liam. 'Be as quick as you can.' He settled his vestments and when he looked down the church over a hundred pairs of astonished eyes stared back at him.

In the vestry, Liam opened the wine cabinet, removed a half-full bottle of altar wine and filled the wine cruet. He was about to put the cork back into the bottle when he wondered what altar wine might taste like. He smelt the wine, put the bottle to his lips and took a good swallow. He liked the taste, so he took a second swallow and then a third.

At the Consecration the priest genuflected and Liam realised the bell he was supposed to ring was on the other side of the altar. He ran to the bell and grabbed it; the sudden snatch caused the bell to peal loudly and Father Keogh scowled harshly at Liam. The boy's heart started to beat faster and the wine started to slosh around in his stomach. Specks of light danced in front of him; he reached out to touch the light and then everything slowly went black. When the bell smashed to the floor the congregation looked up and, to their dismay, the altar boy collapsed.

When Liam opened his eyes he was looking through a grey mist at a beautiful lady in white.

'Are you an angel?' asked the boy.

'No Liam, I'm the bride. We're in the vestry. You fainted, you poor thing. Drink this glass of water.'

'Is the Mass over?' he asked taking a sip of the water.

'Not yet,' replied the groom.

'Then I better get back out there,' said the pale-faced boy.

'No, you stay here and rest,' the bride said softly, and she and her almost-husband left the vestry.

Liam sat and listened to the organ playing in the church. He drank some more water, stood up and walked about the vestry. When he felt well enough he quietly opened the vestry door and walked unsteadily back to the main altar. The bride saw him, smiled, got to her feet and started to applaud. The groom joined his new bride and then as one the congregation rose and applauded, Liam turned to the congregation and bowed gracefully. Father Keogh's eyes flicked upwards, and he gave the final blessing.

'Congratulations,' Liam said to the groom after he signed the register in the vestry. 'Did I do a good job?'

'It was quite an experience,' replied groom. 'If I ever marry again I'll make sure you're the Mass server.'

When the wedding party left the vestry Liam approached Father Keogh.

'How did I do?' asked Liam.

The priest looked questioningly at the boy. He remembered how Liam had forgotten the holy water bucket and the aspergillum and filled the bucket with tap water. He remembered how he had almost forgotten to open the altar gates and how he had caused the water sprinkler to fall to the ground. He remembered how the boy had forgotten to check that the cruets were filled, how he had dropped the altar bell and finally how the groom had to carry the unconscious child into the vestry. Father Keogh took a deep breath, looked into the boy's honest, wide-eyed expectant face and said, 'for a first nuptial Mass, you...you did a good job.'

A smiling Liam left the vestry. The priest bowed his head and hoped God would forgive his white lie.

CHAPTER 15

ÚNA AND HER BOYS

Part 1

The evening sun invaded the Avenue and the wet surface of the road glistened as the three young Foley boys walked home from their matinee visit to the Bohemian Cinema. The only sounds on the darkening street were their light footsteps and their childish voices.

Stephen, the youngest, ran excitedly along the footpath re-enacting a scene from the film they had seen, *Tarzan and the Leopard Woman.*

'Tarzan's great,' Stephen said as he skipped backwards in front of his brothers. 'Ahhhh,' he shouted and beat his chest.

'Stop doing that, you look stupid,' Peter said and made a swipe at his seven-year-old brother. Peter was the eldest of the Foley boys. He was the biggest eleven year old on the Avenue, some of the children called him "Giant", though not to his face.

Stephen jumped on nine-year-old Joseph's back. The two blond-haired boys bounced off a wall and fell to the ground. Peter grabbed his siblings by the collars of their jackets and pushed them against the wall.

'If you two don't behave I'm never going to take you to the pictures again. Now walk properly.'

When the boys reached Number Twenty Five, Peter placed his key in the hall door, opened it and his two younger brothers clattered into the house.

'No messin',' Peter shouted after them.

Stephen jumped up, flicked on the light and the bare electric light that hung from the living room ceiling burst into its sixty watts of luminescence.

The house smelt of furniture polish, a turf fire and yesterday's stew. The living room was where the family ate, read, played cards, listened to the radio and said the rosary. It was where the fire was located and consequently the only room in the house that was regularly warm. Over the fireplace hung a large picture of the Sacred Heart and in the alcove, to the left of the fireplace, hung a picture of St John Bosco. In the alcove on the other side of the fireplace, sitting on a high table, was a wooden Phillips radio. Facing the fireplace was a glass case that housed Mother's treasured Waterford crystal glasses and a few other precious items. Opposite the window was a sideboard and above that was the family altar, on which stood a luminous statue of the Blessed Virgin, a small dome that sheltered a flickering red cross, a white candle and a box of matches.

'Let's play Tarzan,' Stephen said, taking off his overcoat and flinging it on a chair.

'No, we have to get the house ready for Ma. Hang up your coat in the hall,' said Peter.

'I want to play.'

'Play later Stephen, do what you're told. When you've hung up your coat, set the table. Joseph, this place is freezing, get some turf and sticks and build up the fire.'

'How come you're the boss?' asked Stephen.

'Because I am the boss.'

Peter removed a sack of potatoes from under the sink in the kitchen and started to peel them. Joseph went to the coal shed and part-filled the coal scuttle with coal, a few sods of turf and a handful of sticks. Stephen begrudgingly hung up his coat, cleared the table, and took an oilcloth out of the sideboard.

Carrying a half-filled coal-scuttle, Joseph stepped back into the kitchen.

'Didn't break your back did you?' said Peter looking at the half-empty bucket.

'Don't worry, *Giant*,' answered Joseph cheekily, knowing Peter hated his nickname.

'Don't call me that,' Peter said and made a swipe at his brother, who scurried into the living room only to see Stephen standing on the table, reaching for the bare bulb hanging from the ceiling.

'What are you doing?' cried Joseph.

'I'm going to swing on the wire like Tarzan did in the film.'

'Don't!'

Stephen grabbed hold of the lighting fixture; it sparked, ripped out of the ceiling and plunged the house into darkness. The light bulb shattered on the floor. Stephen's body bounced off the table, then the floor and with a thump the table toppled over on top of him. Peter raced into the dark living room, collided with Joseph and crashed to the floor.

'Stephen, Joseph are yous alright?' he cried, scrambling to his feet in the dark.

'No, I'm not,' groaned Stephen from under the table. 'I hurt my arm and my knee.'

'Everyone stay where you are,' said Peter. 'I'm going to get matches.'

'Stephen, Ma is going to kill you for wrecking the place,' complained Joseph getting to his feet.

Peter struck a match; he reached up to the small altar, took down the candle and holder and lit the candle. Ghostly shadows danced on the wall.

'I'm scared of those things,' whispered Stephen, as Joseph lifted the table off his small body.

'They're only shadows,' Joseph said, and looked at his brother's knee. 'Your knee is skinned.'

'Jasus! The place is covered in glass,' said Peter in despair. 'The table is broke. I can't believe this.'

'No, it is not broke, it's fine,' said Joseph 'But look at the wire hanging down the wall.' He pointed at the exposed electric cable. 'That's really broke.'

'Don't touch that, it could kill you!' said Peter.

'Can we fix it?' asked Stephen.

'No we can't. Ma is going to kill us. We're really, really in trouble. Peter, what are we going to do?' asked Joseph.

Peter thought for a moment, then decided. 'We have to leave home. Get some bags and put your stuff in them, and hurry.'

'But I don't want to leave home,' said Stephen.

'Then you can stay and tell Ma you broke the light and destroyed the house.'

'I'm not staying on my own!'

'Then get packing,' snapped his eldest brother.

'What kind of bags?' asked Joseph.

'Any kind of bags, hurry up, Ma will be home soon.'

The only bags the boys could find were brown paper bags. Each boy filled two of them with what he considered his most valued and important possessions. Joseph packed one with clothes, underwear and socks and the other with toys. Stephen packed two bags of toys and Peter shoved jumpers and trousers into one bag and his science fiction books in the other. The three brothers put on their heavy winter overcoats, said goodbye to the house and walked down the Avenue.

When they turned the corner, they stopped. Standing in front of them in her well-worn woollen overcoat and colourful scarf was their mother.

'Hello Ma,' said Stephen meekly.

Úna Foley looked at the faces of her children and knew something was very wrong.

'It was his fault,' Joseph said pointing at Stephen.

'Well, you see Ma, Stephen ...' Peter began.

'Don't say another word, turn around and walk home,' Úna said as calmly as she could.

'Ma, Stephen ...'

'Joseph. We don't discuss family business on the Avenue.'

Peter knew it was pointless to argue; he turned and began his walk home. Joseph and Stephen followed and the family of four walked up the Avenue. Úna Foley opened the door of their home but unusually, the boys did not rush into the house. Úna stepped into the hall, switched on the hall light and nothing happened. She walked up the dark hall where a light flickering in the living room caused her to stop.

'Is there a candle burning?' Úna Foley said, and turned to her children. 'You left the house with a candle burning, what kind of eejits am I rearing?' The children shuffled about looking at each other. Úna walked around the living room and the sound of glass crunched under her feet. 'Jesus, Mary and Joseph, look at the place, it looks like a bomb hit it. What happened?'

'Well, eh...' stuttered Peter.

'First, are you all, alright?'

The three boys nodded meekly.

'Now tell me what happened?'

'We went to the pictures,' said Peter.

'I know that much.'

'*Tarzan and the Leopard Woman* was on,' Stephen said, momentarily excited. 'It was great.'

'What happened here?'

'When we came back...' Peter said, still not looking at his mother.

'Stephen got up on the table and tried to swing from the light,' Joseph interjected, the words spilling out of his mouth in such a rush he forgot to breathe.

'Mother of God you could have been electrocuted, you could have been killed.'

'I'm sorry,' said Stephen.

Úna lifted the burning candle off the altar and surveyed the room.

'I didn't mean it, Ma,' said Stephen.

'You never mean it,' Úna said. 'I honestly don't know what to do with you all. Sometimes I think you would be better off in an orphanage.'

'Please, don't talk about orphanages Ma,' Peter said in a terror-filled voice. 'Stephen didn't mean it, he's just stupid.'

'We'll clean up everything,' Joseph said. 'It will be alright. We'll fix everything.'

A wave of exhaustion swept over Úna; the loss of her husband, the loneliness, the rearing of three boys, the lack of money, the rationing and the sheer hard grind of day-to-day living over-whelmed her. She placed the candle on the sideboard, untied her scarf, took off her coat and sat. The boys gathered anxiously around her.

'I'm a widow, I'm on my own and I'm doing my best. Why are you destroying the little we have?' She slapped Stephen on the head.

Joseph tittered nervously.

'What are you laughing at?' Úna barked and slapped him.

Both boys started to cry. Their mother placed her arms around her sobbing children and held them close. After a minute she stood, took the candle off the sideboard and went into the hall.

Standing on a chair she removed a fuse and replaced it with a spare one. The lights in the hall and the kitchen flickered into life and the spill of light illuminated the living room. She looked at the upturned table, the naked wire hanging down the wall and the glass on the floor and closed her eyes.

'Jesus, you three made a right mess. Peter, get your flashlight, then go to my room and get my bedside lamp. Joseph and Stephen sit on the stairs and don't say a word.'

Úna swept the floor and when Peter returned with the lamp he joined his brothers on the stairs. Úna placed the lamp on top of the radio, plugged it into the wall socket and the room was bathed in yellow light.

'You're not going to put us into an orphanage are you, Ma?' Joseph asked, his eyes glistening with tears.

'No, I am not. I only said that because I was angry. I shouldn't have said it, it was wrong, I'm sorry. Where were you three going when I met you on the street?'

'We don't know,' Peter said.

Joseph and Stephen shrugged their shoulders.

'I'll tell you where you were going, nowhere. You were going nowhere because there is nowhere for you to go. I am a widow, your father is dead and no one in this world will help you except me. We have each other and that is all. I have you and God help you, you have me and it ends there. There is no one else. Now remember this, no matter what happens, we never walk out on each other, we stick together and we face things together. Now go upstairs and not a sound out of you. I'll call you when your food is ready.'

The three boys clambered up the stairs. Halfway up, Stephen stopped and said, 'I didn't mean it Ma.'

'I know you didn't, go on up.'

The following day, wearing his customary baggy corduroy pants, collarless shirt and well-worn woollen sweater, Uncle Martin, Úna's unmarried brother-in-law and self-proclaimed electrician extraordinaire, came with his toolbox and fixed the ceiling light. When the work was completed Martin was given a ham sandwich, a cup of tea and a slice of apple tart, then he went home to his mother's house and ate dinner.

ÚNA AND HER BOYS

Part 2

The shorter days of autumn had arrived and the golden October light was fading as Jacinta Kelly swaggered up the Avenue. Jacinta was Úna's younger sister and they were as different from each other as could be. Jacinta's hair was blonde and long while Úna's was black, short and shiny. Jacinta's clothes were fashionable, flamboyant and a size too small, while Úna's clothes were sensible, neat and, if a little shabby, they were practical and comfortable. Tom Leahy, the paunchy local insurance man, saw Jacinta walking up the Avenue and waved to her. Jacinta stopped, leaned against the wall and waited for him to plod his way over to her.

'How are you Tom, you're not going to ask me out again are you?'

'I never asked you out,' replied a concerned Tom.

'I know Tom, everyone knows you fancy Úna. Are you going to ask her out again?'

'That's what I wanted to talk to you about. Do you think she would go to The Insurance Association's Annual Dress Dance with me? I'm on the shortlist for the association's Salesman of the Year award.'

'She went with you to the Queen's Theatre, so why wouldn't she go to a dress dance with you? But listen, Tom, when you ask Úna to the dress dance, leave out the stuff about the best salesman of the year.'

'Do you think now would be a good time to ask?'

'No, it's a terrible time, the kids nearly destroyed the house the other day.

Come on Friday, after nine, when the kids are asleep and bring a few chocolates. Úna loves Black Magic,' Jacinta said and winked conspiratorially at him.

'Is it you or Úna that likes the chocolates?'

'Bring the chocolates, Tom,' Jacinta said and, with her hips swaying provocatively, she walked slowly up the Avenue.

The chilly white afternoon sun shone brightly on Joseph and Stephen as they fished for pinkeens in the small stream at the back of Mountjoy Prison. Joseph looked at the solitary Pinkeen swimming in his two-pound jam jar and decided, against his mother's explicit instructions, to go and fish in the canal.

'Come on, Stephen, let's go get some real fish.'

The two boys picked up their jackets, jam jars, and their fishing nets and walked the short distance to the canal bank. Joseph dipped his new four-foot-bamboo fishing net into the canal and pulled it through the water. He caught two precious pinkeens right away. Stephen pulled Peter's old tattered net through the water and as quickly as the tiny fish entered the net they exited it.

Half an hour later Joseph admired his catch.

'Look Stephen, that one is a fast swimmer, and that one is fat. Look at the size of him.'

'He's not so fat,' said Stephen, eyeing Joseph's jam jar.

'Did you not catch any fish?'

'My net is full of holes.'

'Do you want to try my net?'

Stephen grabbed the net off the ground, raced to the waterside and plunged it into the canal. When Joseph finished admiring his catch he joined his brother at the water's edge.

'Still no fish?'

'No, my arms are not as long as yours, so I can't lean out as far as you. All the bloomin' fish are in the middle of the canal.'

'I have an idea. If I hold your hand you'll be able to lean out and you'll catch loads of fish.'

Stephen took Joseph's hand, leaned out and pulled the net through the water. When he looked at his net he frowned.

'I need to get out further,' Stephen said, repositioning his feet closer to the edge.

'No, Stephen don't. I won't be able to hold on to you and you could fall in.'

'I'll be alright.'

'You won't be alright, you can't swim.'

Stephen stood close to the canal edge. Joseph took his brother's hand and Stephen moved the net through the water; still no success. He moved closer to the water's edge and leaned out. Joseph felt his fingers slip a little, he tightened his grip but the slipping continued. Their hands separated, Joseph fell backwards and Stephen plunged into the cold canal water.

Joseph looked around for help; they were alone. He reached out to grab Stephen but his brother was too far from the canal bank. Flapping frantically and gulping in mouthfuls of canal water, Stephen shouted for help. Joseph held his bamboo net out to Stephen but he couldn't grasp it. Stephen's head slipped under the water. Joseph stared at the place in the canal where seconds ago his terrified brother had been calling to him. With a splash and gasp, Stephen broke through the surface of the water. Joseph ripped off his pullover and holding onto one arm of it, he threw the pullover to his brother. After two failed attempts Stephen grabbed hold of the pullover and Joseph pulled him to safety.

'I thought you were a goner,' Joseph said between wheezes and gasps.

'So did I,' replied a shivering, white-faced Stephen.

'You were dead lucky.'

'I'm freezing,' Stephen said as his body shuddered.

'Yea, we better go home and dry you off.'

'I can't go home like this?'

'You have to. We'll run, the running will warm you up.'

The white light of the sun was fading as the boys ran along the canal bank to Cross Guns Bridge. People stopped and stared at the soaking-wet, pale-faced and shivering boy running along the street in squelching Wellington boots. At Doyle's Corner, they stopped and Stephen tried to catch his breath.

'Stephen, what happened to you, you're soaking wet,' Uncle Martin said when he walked out of the pub and saw his two nephews.

'He fell into the canal,' said Joseph.

'Not the brightest thing to do, hop up on the crossbar of my bike and I'll bring you home. Joseph, you run alongside us.'

<hr />

Peter was sitting at the fire lost in the adventures of his favourite Eagle comic hero Dan Dare when his mother called downstairs to him.

'I told them to be home half an hour ago. Where in God's name are those brothers of yours?'

'I told you, they went fishing,' replied Peter, barely lifting his eyes out of his comic.

A loud knocking on the front door further interrupted his peace.

'Peter, will you go answer the door, if it's your Aunt Jacinta, tell her I'll be down in a minute.'

'Why do I have to do everything around here,' Peter grumbled, stamping down the narrow hall. When he opened the door and saw a grinning Uncle Martin, a frowning Joseph and a soaking wet Stephen, his mouth fell open.

'What happened, you look like a drowned rat?'

'I fell into the canal,' Stephen said as he pushed past his brother.

'Is that Joseph and Stephen?' Úna called out from the top of the stairs.

'It's me, Martin. I brought the boys home. Stephen fell into the water.'

'Jesus Christ,' Úna said, rushing down the stairs, tying her housecoat around her waist. 'Are you alright love?'

'I'm freezing Ma.'

'Peter go and get two towels. Joseph, are you alright? Where's your pullover?'

'I'm Ok, my pullover's wet,' he replied and held up his pullover.

'Martin thanks very much for looking after the boys. It's good of you,' said Úna, removing Stephen's dripping jumper.

'No thanks necessary, Úna. I'll be off, don't want to be late for my tea. I love your rollers.'

'You don't miss much do you, Martin?' Úna said pulling the rollers out of her hair.

When Martin left, Úna rummaged under the stairs until she found the electric fire they only used in the depths of winter. She switched on the fire and positioned Stephen in front of the two glowing bars of electric heat. Carrying two towels, Peter trundled down the stairs, he threw one towel to Joseph and handed the other to his mother. Úna wrapped the towel around Stephen's head and dried his hair.

'Peter, go up to the bedroom and get some clothes for your brothers. Their pyjamas will do. And clean underwear.'

Grumbling to himself, Peter again pounded up the stairs.

'How in God's name did you manage to get so wet? There's only a drop of water in that stream,' Úna said as she towel dried Stephen's hair. The two boys glanced guiltily at each other. 'You went fishing in the bloody canal, didn't you?' The boys lowered their heads. 'I told you never to go near the canal.'

'Sorry Ma,' said Joseph, his eyes filling with tears.

Úna folded her arms around her wayward sons and hugged them. 'You gave yourselves an awful fright, didn't you? Stephen, you could have been drowned, we could have lost you.'

With tears running down his cheeks, Stephen nodded silently. Peter rushed down the stairs and handed his mother two pairs of pyjamas and underwear. Once she had the boys dry and in their pyjamas, a knock clattered on the front door.

'That's your Aunt Jacinta, Peter, get the door. Why don't you go to bed I'll bring you up some sandwiches later.'

Halfway up the stairs Stephen stopped.

'Ma,' he said with panic in his voice.

'What?'

'We forgot our pinkeens and nets.'

Jacinta had brought a bottle of sherry, and once the boys were settled and fed, Úna took two Waterford glasses from the glass case and Jacinta filled them.

'This is lovely,' Úna said after taking a sip from her glass. 'Jacinta, I don't know what I'd do only for you.'

'And what's a sister for? Drink up, that's the best cream sherry you can get. That's Bristol Cream. I won it at the bingo last week.' Jacinta emptied her glass. 'Did the fixing of the light cost much?'

'No, Martin did it for next to nothing, but I had to ask aul' Quinn next door to return the money she borrowed from me.'

'Kids are expensive,' Jacinta said and refilled their glasses.

'They are, but they're all I've got.'

'And what about me? You have me,' said a slightly annoyed Jacinta.

'I do, you're the only bit of adult company I get. I'm glad to have you, but I do get a bit fed up from time to time.'

'Of course, you do and why wouldn't you, but you are better off than a lot of people. Haven't you got the bit of a job, the widow's pension and don't you make a few bob from the knitting.'

'I do. Why did God have to take George?'

'Ah, don't start that now Úna. I'm not in the mood.' Jacinta rummaged in her handbag, found her lipstick and started to apply it.

'How's the play going that you're in?' Úna asked trying to lift the mood.

'It's not a play, it's an operetta,' Jacinta replied sharply.

'Sorry I can never remember.'

'Well, you should try.'

A loud knock on the front door brought an abrupt end to the sisters' strained conversation.

'That'll be Tom Leahy, Jacinta said getting to her feet. 'He said he'd drop around to ask you to a dress dance. Say yes and I'll get Jock to take me, we'll have a great time. I hope Tom remembers to bring the chocolates.'

Later after Tom left Úna said to her sister, 'I don't know if I should go to the dance, people talk.'

'It's a dress dance, not a weekend in Blackpool. Don't you like Tom?'

'I do, he's nice but still, people talk.'

'You said you'd go now you have to go.'

That night as Úna lay in her bed she thought about her family. She was aware how easy it was for a widow to lose her children. The slightest stain on her character, a perceived impropriety or a bad word from a priest, a holier-than-thou neighbour, a nun, a police-man or even a would-be-do-gooder, could instigate proceedings that could cause a widow to lose her children. The constant aware-ness of people watching and judging her was something she lived with every day and it was as exhausting as it was frightening.

The Kennedy's of Castleross was on the radio and the Foley boys were seated at the living room table eating their dinner of minced beef stew when Peter asked his mother for more.

'There's no more, you've had two helpings. You have a gut like a stocking with a hole in it,' Úna said, clearing Peter's plate off the table.

'I'm still hungry.'

A stone pinged off the living room window. Standing at the wall that separated the garden from the house next door was a large plump woman with shoulder-length brown hair and a merry face. Like many of the women on the Avenue, she looked older than her years.

'That's aul' Quinn,' said Stephen.

'That's Mrs Quinn to you, young man,' corrected his mother.

'She probably wants to borrow money to get her husband's suit out of the pawn,' said Joseph and he giggled.

'Don't say things like that, it's rude,' Úna said sharply.

'You said it yesterday,' said Joseph.

'You're not supposed to repeat everything I say,' she snapped, a little miffed at being caught out. 'Clear off the table boys, I'll be back in a minute.'

She grabbed her purse and went to talk to Mrs Quinn.

'Wait a minute,' Peter said when his mother left the room. 'Are you two finished eating?'

'Yea,' replied the boys.

'Pass them plates over here.'

Joseph and Stephen handed their plates to Peter and he started to eat what was left on them.

'Hey you're eating my dinner,' said Joseph.

'You said you were finished,' replied Peter.

'Well I'm not.'

'Too late.'

'What's a dress dance?' asked Stephen.

'It's when big people get all dressed up and go dancing around,' replied Joseph.

'Dancing around where?'

'I don't know, around.'

'A ballroom, they go dancing around a ballroom,' interjected Peter.

'Why is Ma going dancing around with Mr Leahy?' asked Stephen.

Peter dropped his spoon and Joseph looked at Stephen in astonishment.

'How do you know Ma is going dancing with Mr Leahy?' asked Peter.

'I heard Aunty Jacinta and Ma talking last night when yous were asleep. The dance is in two weeks. Why does Ma want to go dancing?'

'You're too young to understand,' Peter replied, his brow furrowed.

'You always say that when you don't know things,' snapped Stephen.

Úna stood at the four-foot-high wall that separated the two gardens and dug her hands into the pockets of her apron. Mr Quinn assured her that it was an emergency and she would return the ten shillings first thing on Monday morning. The money, Mrs Quinn said, was required to redeem her husband's suit from the pawn-shop so the man would be properly dressed for Sunday Mass. Úna handed Mrs Quinn a ten-shilling note and the money quickly disappeared into the pocket of her hand-knitted cardigan.

'Thanks very much for the few bob. I'll pop down to the pawn this afternoon when himself is having his nap.'

'You're welcome,' Úna said not very sincerely. 'Did your husband get the job you were talking about?'

'Are you joking me, he didn't even go to the interview. He thinks work is an invasion of his privacy.' With a lift of her eyebrow Mrs Quinn changed the conversation. 'I heard you're going to a dress dance with Mr Leahy.'

'Who told you that?'

'Sure you can't draw a breath in these houses without everyone knowing it. Tell us about it.'

'Mrs Quinn, some things are private.'

'I know what you mean. I'm not a gossip, not like Mrs Green.' Mrs Quinn took a deep breath. 'Did you hear what they're saying about Mrs "airs-and-graces" Tyrell?'

'No, I didn't.'

'Well, Mrs Green told me Maisie Rattigan told her that when she was in the butcher's shop she heard Mrs Tyrell ask the butcher for a few bones for the dog.' Mrs Quinn folded her arms, looking superior.

'So?' said Úna.

'She doesn't have a dog, she makes stew with the bones and feeds them to her husband and kids.'

'Yes, well I have to go in, Mrs Quinn. I have to send the boys back to school.'

'Wait a minute, sure I didn't tell you what I called you out to tell you. You know my sister with the back problem,' Mrs Quinn said with a knowing nod.

'Yes, I do.'

'Well, she found this new doctor, a Dr Sol. He's fantastic, wonderful. He cured her.'

'That's marvellous.'

'Foreigners, you can't beat them.'

'I must go, Mrs Quinn.'

'Don't worry about the kids when you go to the dance. I'll keep an ear out for them.'

'Oh thanks, that's very good of you. But Lucy will be looking after them.'

'Then you are going to the dance!'

'Yes, I am,' Úna replied.

'Fair enough, if I can be of any help, just ask.'

ÚNA AND HER BOYS

Part 3

'I know, answer the door,' Peter said when his mother turned to him.

'Thanks, love, I know that knock, that's Lucy,' said Úna.

'Ma my legs hurt,' Stephen said, sitting by the fire.

'Let me see. They look alright, they're not cut or bruised.'

'They hurt,' Stephen murmured.

A smiling Peter walked Aunt Lucy into the living room. Of all Úna's friends, Aunt Lucy was the boys' favourite. She was a small woman who never forgot the children were children.

'Hello, Stephen. Peter told me you had a bit of an adventure recently,' she said as she sat in the chair next to him.

'Yea, I fell into the canal,' he replied. 'I nearly drowned.'

'That must have been frightening, but you're all right now. Úna, I'll look after the boys. Why don't you go upstairs and finish getting ready? Now boys, I brought a little surprise for each of you, but I can't give them to you until you're ready for bed.'

'Thanks, Lucy,' Úna said and climbed the stairs to her bedroom with her blue dress carefully folded over her arm.

Jacinta had spent the last weeks preparing for the dress dance. She'd visited Switzers in Grafton Street and purchased the deepest red lipstick in the shop. She visited Dalton's Hairdressers of Distinction on High Street and had her hair cut and shaped, her eyebrows plucked and her nails manicured. She visited Arnotts of Henry Street and after many hours of agonizing indecision, she decided on a long, yellow, floor-length ball gown, made of taffeta, lace and chiffon. On the night of the dress dance, Jacinta stood in front of the full-length mirror in her bedroom and pronounced herself well pleased with what she saw.

When she and her sometimes boyfriend, Jock Brady, arrived at Number Twenty Five they were in good humour if not a little giddy – they had spent the previous hour in Kavanagh's Select Lounge on Mountjoy Street.

'My Ma wants to know if you want tea,' Peter said, standing in the parlour in front of what he considered a very silly Aunt Jacinta and an overdressed man.

'No thanks, Peter. We've had our tea,' Jacinta said, glancing at Jock and giggling girlishly.

Peter rolled his eyes.

'Are you the eldest of the family?' asked Jock.

'Yes sir, I am. I'm eleven.'

'Nice to meet you, and there's no need to call me sir, I'm not a school teacher.'

'That is certainly true,' Jacinta said and giggled again. 'Peter, would you tell your mother to hurry. Tell her Mr Leahy will be here in a few minutes.'

'All right,' Peter replied, delighted to be able to escape.

Leaning back on the sofa Jock opened his tuxedo and produced a naggin of whiskey. He twisted the cork out of the bottle, took a swig and offered Jacinta the bottle.

'For Christ's sake put that away, you don't want the kids to see us drinking.'

Jock was about to push the cork back into the bottle when Jacinta took it from him, rubbed its rim with the palm of her hand and took a gulp.

'Has Tom being seeing much of Úna?' Jock asked as he returned the bottle to his inside pocket.

'A bit, he works a lot in Cork so he's not in Dublin all that much.'

The parlour door opened and Úna stepped into the room. Her dark, shiny, black hair was cropped elfin style. Her light blue column-shaped dress was long and elegant and dotted with sequins at the neckline. Over her gown, she wore a short white bolero-style jacket.

'May I say you are looking stunning tonight, Úna,' Jock said getting to his feet and giving a little whistle.

'You look wonderful, Úna,' Jacinta said, and jumped up and kissed her sister on the cheek.

Úna beamed, she was proud of her dress and jacket – she had spent many long hours at her sewing machine making them.

'You look like a film star and I feel like a film star,' Jacinta said, and guffawed loudly at her "joke".

'Did you two stop somewhere on the way here?' asked Úna suspiciously.

'Yes, we had a cup of tea at the vicarage,' said Jacinta and gave another big horse laugh.

⇥⇤

Úna's companion for the evening Tom Leahy, walked proudly up the Avenue. He was feeling good; he was wearing his new tuxedo, starched white shirt, black bow tie and patent leather shoes. He was carrying a small bouquet of flowers and another box of Black Magic chocolates. He tapped on the window of Number Twenty Five and Jacinta opened the door.

'I see the riff-raff got here before me,' Tom said, following her into the parlour.

'Mind who you are calling riff-raff,' said Jock.

'Úna, you look beautiful, really beautiful. I love your dress, blue is my favourite colour.' Tom handed Úna the flowers and the chocolates.

'Thank you, Tom, you look very smart yourself.'

'How was your day?'

'Stephen's complaining that his legs hurt, but apart from that everything is fine.'

'Never mind the boys, Úna. Are you ready to have a good night Tom?' asked Jacinta.

'I am. I don't know if you know it but I'm up for Salesman of the Year and I'm told I have a good chance of winning it.'

'We do know it, because you've told us a million times,' said Jacinta, rolling her eyes again.

'Great, if everyone is ready we should go,' Jock said getting to his feet. He handed Jacinta her coat, Úna popped her head into the living room and said goodnight to her boys.

'Goodnight, Ma,' the boys called back.

'Enjoy yourself,' said Lucy with a smile.

'Yes, let's go Úna or the night will be over before it begins,' Jock said buttoning his overcoat.

When Úna, Jacinta, Tom and Jock arrived at the Metropole Ballroom the dance was already in progress. The ballroom was thronged with people drinking and laughing. A huge banner draped across the front of the bandstand welcomed everyone to *The Insurance Association of Ireland's Annual Dress Dance 1950*. Chatting excitedly like schoolgirls, the two sisters made their way through the noisy throng to the ladies room, while Tom and Jock stood at the table plan and looked for their table's location.

'There we are, up on the balcony,' said Tom.

When the sisters joined them at the bar, the men were halfway through their pints of Guinness. Úna felt wonderful, for the first time in a long time she felt free. She enjoyed the meal of roast chicken and ham. As she sat back in her chair she sipped her coffee and her eyes roved aimlessly over the sea of dancers on the floor. She loved seeing the smiling faces of the women in their beautiful dresses and coiffed hair. She enjoyed looking at the jovial faces of the men in their elegant black tuxedoes. The throaty singing of Peggy Dell and the jazzy sound of the Earl Gill Band filled her with delight; she felt young and alive.

Sitting across from Úna Tom smiled as he watched the two sisters chatting and talking. Tom liked Úna, he liked her honest face and gentle smile. He thought of her as a happy, innocent, almost childlike, creature. But he was aware that, in the blink of an eye, she could transform into an intensely protective mother. He shook his head, he did not want to think of her like that, not tonight; tonight he wanted to think of her as a young woman and his dancing partner.

Standing at the bar, Jock Brady ordered two pints and, as the bartender poured the pints, he admired a passing woman. 'Nice looking lady you brought to the dance,' he said to Tom as they waited patiently for their pints to settle. 'Makes me think I'm with the wrong sister. I've seen many an eye thrown in her direction tonight.'

'Yes. Úna is looking particularly pretty this evening,' replied Tom.

'I have to say, I admire you, not many men would take on three kids.'

'How are you and Jacinta getting along?' Tom replied, deliberately changing the conversation.

'That, my friend, is a long story that I'm not going to bore you with tonight.'

At the table, Jacinta placed her hand on Úna's.

'How are you and Tom getting along?'

'How much have you had to drink, Jacinta?'

'Not enough. Tell me, do you fancy Tom or not?' Jacinta lit another cigarette.

'He's nice and yes, I am enjoying myself.'

'Tom is nice but he is a bit boring.'

'I don't find him boring, perhaps a little serious and quiet, but that's nice.'

'So you like him?'

'I do. How are you and Jock getting along these days?'

'Same as usual, I like him but as he says himself, he likes variety.'

When the MC announced the winner of *The Salesman of the Year 1950* was Tom Leahy, Úna, Jacinta, Jock and the entire ballroom erupted in applause. A beaming Tom embraced Úna. He accepted his prize and made the short speech he had spent hours preparing. When he returned to the table with the trophy, the bandleader announced the last dance of the evening. Tom took Úna's hand and led her to the middle of the empty dance floor.

'Let's show them how it's done,' he said, as he placed his hand on her waist.

'Very well Mr Astaire, lead the way.'

'I'll have you know I'm more than a pretty face.'

'I know you are, and I like your face.'

Úna and Tom danced the quickstep and when the tempo changed to a slow foxtrot they danced intimately.

The taxi stopped outside Number Twenty Five and a smiling Úna and a light-hearted Tom stepped out of the cab. Tom handed the *Salesman of the Year* trophy to Úna and paid for the taxi. Then he slipped his arm around her and kissed her gently on the cheek.

'Stop it, Tom,' Úna whispered. 'The neighbours will talk.'

'It's two o'clock in the morning, they're all asleep.'

'How was your evening?' Lucy asked when Úna and Tom walked into the living room.

'It was lovely,' said Úna. 'All quiet upstairs?'

'Not a whisper all night.'

As Úna slipped upstairs to check on her boys, Lucy turned to Tom. 'Congratulations on the award. You know it's lovely to see Úna so happy. It's a long time since I saw her smile like that. It's not every man that would ...' Lucy looked up as she heard Úna's footsteps on the stairs. 'I set a small fire in the parlour for you both, go in. I'll bring in some tea to you.'

Úna blushed. 'Such treatment, I feel like I'm the lady of the manor.'

'You are the lady of the manor,' Tom declared. He took Úna's arm and escorted her into the parlour. 'I had a wonderful evening, my lady.'

'So did I, kind sir, I didn't realise you were such a good dancer,' Úna said, settling her dress.

'You made me look good,' said Tom, posing proudly by the fireplace, his elbow on the mantelpiece.

The parlour door opened and Lucy entered carrying a tray of tea and cake.

'There you are, I'll be off now,' she said, as she placed it on the parlour table. 'I'm going to leave you young people to yourselves.'

'It's a bit late, would you like me to walk you home?' Tom asked, clearly hoping she'd say no.

'Don't be silly, I'm only around the corner. Oh, Úna, Stephen said his leg was hurting him, but it didn't stop him falling asleep.'

'I'm sure he'll have forgotten all about it by morning.'

'Right, I'm off. Goodnight Tom, see you Úna,' Lucy said and closed the door behind her.

Tom sat beside Úna on the couch. 'Did you enjoy the evening?'

'I did, Mr Leahy, I had a lovely time thank you.'

He took her in his arms and kissed her. He was about to kiss her a second time when there was a cry from the bedroom.

Úna broke free. 'That's Stephen.'

'He'll be all right.'

Úna flashed him a disapproving look. 'I'll only be a minute.'

'Really, a minute?'

'Don't. I'll be as quick as I can.'

She hurried up to the boys' bedroom. Peter and Joseph were fast asleep but Stephen was sitting up and weeping gently. Úna sat on the bed and placed her arms around her son. 'There, there love.' Stephen wrapped his arms around his mother and snuggled into her. 'What's the matter, love?'

'My legs hurt.'

Úna turned on the bedside lamp, pulled back the covers, pushed up the legs of Stephen's pyjamas and examined his legs and feet.

'Everything looks fine, there are no marks, the skin is not broken and there's not even a little scratch. Where exactly does it hurt?'

'All over.'

'Would you like to try to walk?'

'No.'

'I want you to try.'

Úna lifted Stephen's legs out of the bed and placed them on the floor. With help, Stephen managed to get to his feet but when Úna stood away from him he collapsed.

'What's going on?' asked a sleepy Joseph rubbing his eyes.

'Stephen is on the floor. Help me lift him into his bed.'

Joseph stumbled out of his bed and took hold of his brother's legs. Úna placed her hands under his arms and they attempted to lift him back onto the bed, but the weight was too great for Joseph and Stephen fell back onto the floor.

They were about to attempt a second time when Tom appeared at the bedroom door. He stepped across the bedroom, lifted Stephen and placed him in his bed.

'Sorry love,' Úna said, rubbing the child's hand.

'What's wrong with my legs, why are they not working?'

'I don't know love. I'll have to get the doctor. Joseph get back into bed.'

'What's going on?' groaned Peter, rubbing his eyes.

'Don't get up, Peter, everything's fine.' She kissed the boys and followed Tom downstairs. 'You'll have to leave, Tom. I'm sorry the evening ended this way but I have to fetch the doctor.'

'Why didn't you ask me to help?'

'If you have to be asked to help, you don't want to help.'

'That's unfair,' replied a visibly hurt Tom.

'I'm sorry, I didn't mean that. I'm upset.'

Tom fell silent, and then with great resignation said, 'No, you stay. Is Dr Malone your doctor?' Úna nodded. 'I'll go get him.'

'Tom, I'm sorry what I said.'

'You have more to be worrying about than my feelings.' Tom put on his coat and without saying another word left the house.

'Am I going to be all right?' Stephen asked when Úna returned to his bedside.

'Yes, you are. Tom is gone for the doctor and he won't be long. Boys, let's say a rosary while we're waiting on the doctor.'

Peter and Joseph made a face at each other. Úna went to her bedroom for her rosary beads. When she returned she knelt by Stephen's bed, draped her rosary beads around her fingers, made the sign of the cross and recited the first half of a *Hail Mary*; she paused and the three boys raggedly recited the second half of the prayer. They were on the tenth decade when Dr Malone arrived.

'Well young man, what's your name and what ails you?' the doctor asked in his rumbling deep voice.

'Stephen Foley is my name and my legs hurt.'

'Well, I better have a look at them.' The doctor turned to Úna. 'While I'm examining the boy would you be so good as to make me a cup of tea.'

Dr Malone was a tall, gruff man of great authority. He had grey hair and an enormous forehead and children greatly feared him and his needles. Downstairs, Úna put the kettle on the gas stove and was setting the table when she noticed Tom's trophy sitting on the sideboard. It was only then she realised he had not returned with the doctor. She sat at the table and wondered what might have been.

A few minutes later Dr Malone trotted down the stairs and sat at the fire warming his hands.

'Well? What's wrong with Stephen?' Úna asked, as she poured tea.

'Well, I can't tell you very much right now. I gave him something to help him sleep so he'll be all right for the night. I want you to take him to the Mater Hospital tomorrow, they'll run some tests. Is this for me?' the doctor asked, looking at the cup of tea. Úna nodded and the doctor put a spoonful of sugar into the cup. 'It's all very strange, only I know Stephen was vaccinated I'd say he's showing early signs of polio.'

Úna's stomach tightened and bile rose in her throat.

'Stephen wasn't vaccinated against polio. Peter and Joseph were, but Stephen was sick the day he was supposed to be vaccinated.'

Dr Malone placed his cup and saucer on the table.

'Mrs Foley, I shouldn't have said that, it was idle speculation, it meant nothing.'

'If it meant nothing why did you say it?'

'Mrs Foley, it's late I should be off. Have Stephen at the Mater Hospital at noon tomorrow.' He wrote a note and handed it to her.

'I'll make the necessary arrangements with the hospital and try not to worry.'

'How can I not worry? I'm sorry, you're right doctor, it's late, thank you for coming.'

'Goodnight Mrs Foley, I'll let myself out. Oh, by the way, Mr Leahy said he'll drop by tomorrow to pick up his trophy.'

Úna sat in her beautiful dress, looked into the fires dying embers and wondered what it would be like if her husband was alive. When Stephen cried out for her again, she turned out the light and walked up the stairs.

ÚNA AND HER BOYS

Part 4

Bright morning sunlight shone on the snow-covered roofs of the houses on Phibsboro Road, the morning Úna visited Dr Malone's surgery. Dark and serious, the doctor sat behind his desk and told Úna that Stephen's hospital test results were inconclusive and that further tests were necessary.

'What kind of tests?' asked Úna.

'Tests that can only be conducted in the Polio Clinic.' The doctor leaned back in his chair. 'Unfortunately, they won't be able to see him for six months. They've put him on the waiting list. They'll be in touch as soon as an appointment can be arranged.'

'Six months wait for an appointment? In the meantime what is to happen to my son?'

'Mrs Foley, I'm sorry. You'll just have to wait.'

⟩⟨ ⟨⟩

The following morning was freezing. A cold, silvery light sliced through the living room window as Joseph and Peter raced down the stairs. When they finished their breakfast, Úna handed each boy his overcoat, school cap and schoolbag.

'Say goodbye to your brother,' Úna said, as the boys swung their schoolbags onto their backs.

'Bye Stephen,' Joseph shouted up the stairs. 'When will he be coming back to school?'

'When the doctor says he can,' said Úna.

'Ma, some of the boys in my class say he'll never get better,' Peter said with a finality that shocked Úna.

'Don't listen to them. What do those eejits know?'

'Ma, some of the boys in my class say polio can't be cured,' said Joseph.

'Stephen has not got polio.'

'But Dr Malone said he did,' said Joseph.

'No, he didn't, he said Stephen might have polio but we have to wait until the clinic sees him.'

A pebble pinged on the living room window and Joseph looked out to the garden.

'Mr Quinn must need his suit for Mass,' sniggered Joseph.

'Joseph, I told you before not to talk about the neighbours like that.'

'But it's true,' said Joseph.

'Bye Ma,' said, Peter. 'See you, Stephen.'

Joseph kissed his mother on the cheek. 'Race you, Peter,' he said, as he pushed his big brother into the parlour and fled.

Scrambling wildly, Peter rushed down the hall after Joseph. Úna shook her head, took her purse from her handbag and went out to the garden.

'Mrs Foley, isn't this weather brutal,' Mrs Quinn said, brushing snow off the top of the separating wall.

'It's dreadful. Mrs Quinn, I haven't got much time, I have to get back to Stephen.'

'Sure isn't that what I called you for. I heard you up in the middle of the night. I knew something was wrong so I made something for you and the little tyke.'

Mrs Quinn placed an apple tart on the top of the wall.

'Thanks very much, that's very good of you. Stephen loves apple tart.'

'What did the doctor say was wrong with him?'

'He said he doesn't know. He has to undergo more tests.'

'Let's hope it's nothing serious, himself is not so well, I think he got a bad pint somewhere. He's in a terrible state, puking up all night.'

'Sorry to hear that,' Úna said and wondered how Mr Quinn managed to get a bad pint nearly every weekend. 'You called me out, did you want to tell me something?'

'Yes, it's something I'd like to clear up. You know that ten shillings you borrowed from me on Monday, could I have it back please.'

'What do you mean, have it back?'

'It's my money and I'd like to have it back.'

'Mrs Quinn, you never loaned me money. You borrowed ten shillings from me and you paid it back to me. I've never borrowed money from you.'

'I see. Well then, can you lend me ten shillings?'

Úna removed a ten-shilling note from her purse and handed it to Mrs Quinn.

'Give it back to me first thing Monday morning.'

'I will, of course, don't I always?'

'Mrs Quinn, your sister, the one who had pains in her back, how is she?'

'She's great, back to her old self. She went to the bingo the other night, didn't win anything.'

'Who was that doctor that attended her?'

'I don't remember his name. No, I'm telling a lie, I remember. His name is Dr Sol and he works in the Richmond Hospital. He's a great doctor, a real gentleman.'

'Do you think he might have a look at Stephen?'

'I'm sure he would. I'll be seeing my sister this afternoon and I'll get her to ask the doctor to drop around.'

'Thanks very much, Mrs Quinn, I'm much obliged to you.'

'Not at all, Mrs Foley. You know, them foreign doctors are great. They know voodoo and everything.'

Mrs Quinn turned abruptly and left Úna standing at the wall wondering what kind of doctor was going to attend to her son.

After school, Joseph and his friend, Johnny Farrell, went to the nearby park for a football kick-about. The boys were enjoying their game when the terrors of the Avenue, the pimple-faced eleven-year-old Anto Ryan and his lumpy-looking friend Jacko Byrne sauntered into the park. Anto intercepted the ball and kicked it to his friend Jacko. Joseph and Johnny tried to retrieve the ball but Anto and his friend were bigger, more skilled and they easily prevented the ball from returning to its owner.

'Give us our ball back,' said an annoyed Joseph, after a third unsuccessful attempt to reclaim it.

'Take it, if you can,' laughed Anto.

'Give us the ball or we'll get the Giant to get it for us,' shouted Johnny.

'Oh I'm scared, I'm really scared. I'm quaking in my boots, the Giant is coming,' sneered Anto.

Joseph rushed for the ball. Anto waited until Joseph was upon him and kicked his shin. Joseph fell to the ground and Anto bounced the ball off his head.

'You can tell the Giant that we're not frightened of him,' Anto scoffed as Joseph lay on the ground trying hard not to cry.

A folded woollen blanket covered part of the living room table on which Úna ironed Joseph's school shirt. Peter was sitting at the other end of the table, engrossed in a science fiction novel, when there was a knock on the front door.

'Answer that, Peter,' Úna said without looking up.

'Ah, Ma.'

Úna shot a stormy look at her eldest son and he begrudgingly rose. A minute later an astonished Peter rushed back into the living room and uncharacteristically closed the door behind him.

'Ma, there's a black man in a suit at the door.'

Úna rested the iron, cracked open the door and peeped down the hall.

'Jesus, you're right, he is a black man,' she said quietly to Peter.

'Mrs Foley?' asked the man with a little wave.

'Yes?' Úna said, walking down the hall brushing imaginary dust off her apron. 'What can I do for you?'

'I'm Dr Sol,' the man replied. Úna cocked her head to one side. 'Mrs Quinn's sister said your son was ill.'

'Oh, Dr Sol,' Úna said, suddenly remembering the conversation she had with Mrs Quinn.

'May I come in?'

'Oh yes, please do, I'm so sorry.'

Carrying a well-worn leather bag, Dr Sol walked briskly down the hall and into the living room. Peter couldn't take his eyes off the first black person to ever enter his home.

'Close your mouth Peter,' Úna said as she walked past her eldest son.

A furious Joseph and an angry Johnny were walking home through the Blessington Basin when they heard Anto and Jacky running after them.

'Don't you want your ball?' Anto said bouncing the ball off the Basin's high wall.

'Of course I want my ball,' replied Joseph.

'Take it,' Anto said holding it out to Joseph.

Joseph lunged at the ball. Anto pulled it away and Jacko thumped him on the back. Johnny tried to snatch the ball but Jacko shoved him hard and he fell to the ground. Laughing heartily, Anto and Jacko ran off back to the park.

━┼┼━

Úna was tending to the fire and Peter was sitting at the table doing his hated maths homework when Dr Sol came down the stairs, removing the stethoscope from his neck and placing it in his leather bag.

'What do you think, Doctor?' Úna asked drying her hands in a tea towel.

'You said earlier that you don't believe your son has polio?'

Úna nodded.

'Why do you think that?'

Fascinated by the doctor's hands, Peter hadn't taken his eyes off them. He had never seen hands like them; the backs of the doctor's hands were black, jet black, while the palms were pink. Unable to resist the urge to touch them he reached across the table and tapped the doctor's hand.

'The black doesn't come off,' he said, with a note of surprise.

'No, it doesn't, wouldn't it be terrible if it did,' replied the doctor with a joyous laugh. 'I'd never have a clean shirt.'

'Peter you're being very rude,' said Úna.

'He's not being rude, he's just inquisitive and honest,' the doctor said with a smile.

Úna glared at her son and he resumed his homework.

'Young Sean McGuire, who lives a few doors up the Avenue, has polio but his symptoms are nothing like Stephen's.'

'All polio patients don't have the same symptoms.'

'Can you help my son?'

'I can't interfere with another doctor's treatment plan.'

'Doctor Malone hasn't prescribed any medicine for Stephen. He said Stephen has to go to the polio clinic but the clinic can't see him for six months.'

'I see,' the doctor said. He removed a prescription pad from his leather bag, wrote on it, tore off the top sheet and handed it to Úna. 'I'd like to try something.'

'Doctor Malone said there are no medicines for polio,' Úna said looking at the prescription.

'Strictly speaking that is not medicine; it's a prescription for rubbing alcohol. Your son's legs need to be massaged every day.'

'How long will the treatment take?'

'I don't know. Until the polio clinic can see him, perhaps.'

'Doctor, I can't afford to pay for that much treatment.'

'There will be no charge. I'll put it down to research. This is how we will proceed. Tomorrow, I'll message Stephen's legs and I'll teach you how to do it and I'll tell you what to look out for. I will drop by every two weeks or so, and see how things are progressing. What do you say?'

Úna nodded. 'Do you think it will help?'

'There are no guarantees. I will be here tomorrow at half past twelve. Will you have the prescription filled by then?'

'I will.'

The doctor replaced his notepad in his bag.

'Doctor, why are you helping me?'

'Let us say, I have a family back home, and leave it at that.'

'Whatever the reason, thank you,' Úna said, as she walked him to the door. 'Where is your home?'

'Tanzania.'

'Is it a nice place?'

'It is a beautiful land.'

Úna opened the front door and a weeping Joseph crashed past her and ran into the house. Doctor Sol smiled ruefully. Úna shook her head.

'Until tomorrow,' Doctor Sol said.

'Thanks again, Doctor.'

'What happened?' Úna asked when she returned to the living room.

'Me and Johnny were playing football in the park and Anto and Jacko hit us and robbed the ball.'

'Was that the ball Uncle Martin gave us?' asked a suddenly alert Peter.

'It doesn't matter about the ball, what did Anto and Jacko do to make you cry?' asked Úna.

'He kicked me on the shin and bounced the ball off my head and Jacko thumped me on the back.'

'Those boys are blackguards. Does it hurt?'

'Of course it hurts.'

Úna examined Joseph's leg. 'Your shin is skinned. I'll put a dressing on it. Are you sure it wasn't an accident?'

'It wasn't an accident. Anto and Jacko are always picking on me.'

'Don't worry son, it will be all right before you're twice married.'

'I hate when you say that, it's stupid.'

'Ma, I'm going out for a bit.' Peter grabbed his coat and walked up the Avenue. When he arrived at the park, Anto and Jacko were still kicking the ball to each other. Peter leaned against the trunk of an ash tree and waited until Anto and Jacko saw him. Anto picked the ball off the ground and walked over to Peter.

'I was just going to bring the ball down to your house, your brother forgot it,' Anto said holding out the ball to Peter.

'Did he now? Why don't we have a game, just between us?'

'I have to go home, me dinner's ready.'

'I'm sure your Ma won't mind if you're a little late,' Peter said and plunged the ball into Anto's stomach.

'Hey, that hurt.'

'Oh sorry Anto, now I'm going over there and I want you to kick the ball to me.'

'Don't call me Anto, it's not my name.'

'Sorry Turnip Head. What would you like me to call you?'

'Feck off, you don't scare me, *Giant*.'

'Oh Turnip Head, you shouldn't have called me that. That was a very stupid thing to do, Anto.'

'I told you, don't call me Anto.'

Peter placed the ball on the ground, charged at it and kicked it as hard as he could. The ball smashed into Anto's face, he fell backwards, crashed against the park's iron railings and slid to the ground. Before he got back on his feet Peter ran over to him.

'Get up, Turnip Head.'

'Leave me alone,' cried Anto.

'Stay away from my brothers,' Peter said and punched Anto three times in the upper arm, then bounced the ball off his head. 'The next time you touch either of my brothers I'll pull your feckin head off. Now, do you want me to show you how I'd do that?'

'No, I don't.'

'Good, now where's your friend Jacko?' Peter asked and bounced the ball off Anto's head until he answered the question.

───━┤┼├━───

The day's sun had disappeared and a cold moon was illuminating the city as Úna walked home from Dargan's Chemist shop. As she neared the Blessington Basin, a black car pulled up beside her. The car window lowered and a sheepish Tom Leahy looked up at her. It was four weeks since she had seen or heard from Tom. He hadn't collected his precious trophy.

'Want a lift home?' he asked.

'No thanks, I can cut through the Basin, it's much shorter and quicker.'

'I'd like to talk to you, Úna.' His voice was quiet and serious.

Úna's mind was clear and resolved. 'Very well,' she said and sat into the car. Tom turned off the engine, sat back and tapped on the steering wheel.

'I haven't seen you since the dance,' she said. 'Were you ill?'

'No, the company sent me to Cork,' he replied, not looking at her.

'Do they not have telephones or post offices in Cork?'

'Of course, they do.' He turned to her. 'The truth is, I wasn't *sent* to Cork. I requested to be sent there. I needed time to think.'

'What did you need to think about?'

'About us.'

'You needed to go away to think about us?'

'Úna, I like you ... but ... I don't know how to put this ... I don't think I could be a father to another man's children.'

'Well Tom, despite not knowing how to put it, you managed to find the words.' She placed her hand on the door handle. 'Tom it's alright, I understand.'

'No, it's not alright. I feel terrible.'

'Why should you feel terrible? You were nice to me, we went out a few times and we enjoyed ourselves.'

'Úna I like you, I do. I fancy you. But three children? It's an awful lot. If you would consider ...'

'Stop right there, Tom. I don't want to hear any talk like that.'

'If you could see your way to ...'

'I said stop it. There are no ifs or buts in my life. I am a widow with three children and that is not going to change.'

Úna waited on Tom's reply. He bowed his head, glanced at his watch and said 'I'll drop you home.'

'No Tom. I'll walk.'

Úna stepped out of the car and walked into the Basin. Tom remained in the car, staring straight ahead.

It was the 8th of December and the last rays of the day's sun were disappearing from the Avenue. At Number Twenty Five, the Foleys were busily preparing for Christmas. Úna was mixing the Christmas pudding on the living room table. Joseph was rummaging in the box of last year's Christmas decorations trying to find undamaged paper chains to hang in the living room and Peter was arranging Christmas cards on the mantelpiece. Úna poured half of a bottle of stout into the Christmas pudding mix. Peter arrived at his mother's side, slid his hand into the paper bag on the table, removed a handful of raisins and put them in his mouth. Úna thrust her elbow into her son's side.

'Help Joseph with the decorations,' she ordered.

Peter took a chair from the table, set it in a corner and stood on it. Joseph handed him a paper chain and a thumbtack and Peter attempted to pin the decoration to the wall.

'You need to put it up higher,' said Joseph.

'I can't reach any higher, peabrain.'

'Ma, did you hear what he called me?'

'Will you two stop it, it's Christmas. Can you not do one thing together without fighting? You know Santa doesn't come to bold boys.'

'Peabrain, Ma's talking to you. Santa won't be leaving you any presents.'

'Ma?' exclaimed Joseph.

'Peter, for God's sake, stop calling your brother names and stop teasing him.' A loud knock on the front door brought silence to the room. 'Peter that will be your Uncle Martin, go answer the door.'

'Yea, yea, yea,' Peter mumbled to himself as he lumbered down the hall. He pulled open the door and standing on the doorstep with a grin on his face was Uncle Martin.

'How is Ireland's answer to Joe Louis?' Martin snapped into a boxer's fighting position and pretended to throw a punch at his nephew. 'Heard about what you did to Anto, his arm is in a sling.'

Peter grinned and stepped out of the house onto the snowy Avenue.

'Don't say anything to Ma about it. She'll kill me if she finds out.'

'It's just between us, man to man. How is Stephen? Your Ma asked me to drop over to lift him down the stairs.'

'Oh yea, come on in, we're putting up the Christmas decorations. The doctor is upstairs with Stephen.'

Martin walked into the living room and his eyes immediately fixed on the half-full bottle of stout. He walked casually over to the table, picked up the bottle and downed the stout in one swallow.

'Nectar of the Gods,' he said and smacked his lips.

'I wasn't finished with that, you big lug,' said Úna.

'You know Úna, what I always liked about you was your sweet and gentle nature. Is your black man still here?'

'He's not my man and he is upstairs, so keep your voice down.'

'What kind of doctor is he, a witch doctor?'

Joseph and Peter giggled and Úna shook her head in exasperation. 'Shut up and have some manners.'

'Ma, you told Uncle Martin to shut up,' said Joseph.

'Give it a rest Joseph, and finish putting up those decorations. You've been at it for ages. Look at the place.' Then without drawing a breath she continued, 'How is your mother, Martin?'

'Right as rain, how long more is Botswana going to be coming here?'

'Stop talking about the doctor like that. He finishes with the hospital after Christmas and then he's going back to his own country.'

'I know there's nothing to it but people are beginning to talk,' Martin said in a mock gossipy voice. 'A good-looking woman like you ...'

'Martin, don't joke about that.'

'Just repeating what I heard.'

'No, you're not. People are not saying anything like that. It's only you that's saying it. And it isn't funny.'

The bedroom door closed and Doctor Sol came down the stairs.

'Hello Doctor, I hope our snowy winter weather isn't too cold for you,' said Martin.

'Not at all, in my country, it often snows in winter.'

'Oh does it?' Martin replied with little interest.

'Doctor, this is my brother-in-law Martin. He carries Stephen up and down the stairs for me.'

'Pleased to meet you, Martin.'

'Nice to meet you, Doctor. I'll go get Stephen, I don't want to be late for the match,' Martin said and skipped up the stairs.

'Is there any improvement?' asked Úna, leaning on the table.

'Sorry to say there is no change.'

'What about the sensations he feels in his legs?'

'I did some tests but there was no response. The sensations Stephen is experiencing are known as phantom pains, they are imaginary and they are to be expected in situations like these.'

'Then there is no change,' Úna said softly.

'That is correct.'

'Are you still planning on going back home after Christmas?'

'Yes, that is my plan.' The doctor's voice grew serious. 'Mrs Foley even if I was staying, there is little more I could do. But you should keep massaging Stephen's legs, it's good for his circulation.'

'I will. You must be looking forward to seeing your family again.' Úna opened the top drawer in the sideboard, removed a brown paper package and handed it to the doctor. 'I knitted this for your wife, I hope she likes it.'

'There was no need to do that, but thank you so very much.'

Martin carried Stephen down the stairs and placed him in an armchair in front of the fire. Úna stood over him and ran her fingers through the boy's hair.

'Ma, did you see the doctor's new watch, it's deadly. He let me put it on, didn't you, Doctor?'

'Yes, I did.'

'Doc, is that your car outside the door?' asked Martin.

'It is.'

'Nice car, I wonder if you would drop me down to Conway's Pub.'

'I thought you were going to a football match.'

'I certainly am, but I have to have a quick one to get me in the mood, you know yourself?'

'Mrs Foley, I'm sorry I couldn't be of more help,' said the doctor.

'You gave me hope and for that, I'm grateful.'

Martin was standing on the snowy footpath admiring the doctor's car when Dr Sol joined him.

'You wouldn't care to join me in Conway's for a jar, would you?' Martin said as he got into the car.

'Thank you, but I have another patient to visit,' replied the doctor politely.

Úna watched the doctor's car drive down the Avenue; after it turned the corner she returned to the living room. Stephen was sitting by the fire reading a comic, Joseph was tidying up the last of the decorations and Peter was helping himself to some more raisins. Úna looked around the room and smiled.

'The place looks lovely, boys. Let's open a bottle of that Christmas lemonade.'

'Great,' Joseph said, his eyes wide with instant excitement.

'Peter, get four cups and the bottle opener from the kitchen. Joseph, gather up the last of the decorations. I'll get the lemonade and a few custard creams from the parlour. We'll have ourselves a little party.'

She went into the parlour, took a large bottle of Taylor-Keith's red lemonade and a packet of Jacob's Custard Creams from the stock of Christmas treats behind the sofa. Joseph put the box of decorations under the stairs. Peter ran into the kitchen, grabbed four cups from the dresser, then rummaged in the utensil drawer until he found the bottle opener. Stephen, using his hands and arms, swung his body out of the armchair and onto his chair at the table. Úna placed the lemonade and the biscuits on the table and looked at her three boys.

'Ma, can I open the bottle?' asked Peter.

'Yes, Peter, you can, you are the man of the house.'

Peter flipped off the cap and noisily the orange liquid spat, spurted and bubbled down the side of the glass bottle. The boys cheered. Joseph and Stephen held up their cups and Peter poured some sweet, bubbly lemonade into each cup.

'Ma, I got that funny feeling in my legs again,' said Stephen when he finished his lemonade.

'Don't worry love, the doctor said they're phantom pains, he said they'll go away.'

'Ma, tell us about Da again,' asked Joseph.

'Your Da was a very special man and he loved each of you very much.'

'Tell us about when he played the piano,' said Stephen.

'Oh, he could make a piano talk. He would sit at the piano and be the king of the keyboard. Everywhere we went they asked him to play and he loved playing. I think he was happiest when he was playing his music. He used to wink at me when he played, it made me feel so special. Your father was a lovely man. That's why God took him. It's not fair, but there is nothing we can do about that. It's Christmas, let's be happy, Peter give us a song.'

Peter stood in front of the fire; the room quietened and in his boy soprano voice he sang Gounod's *Ave Maria*, then Joseph put on his gloves and sang *Burlington Bertie from Bow*. Next to sing was Stephen and his song was *How Much is that Doggie in the Window* and Úna sang, *She Moved through the Fair*.

The window ledge was rimmed with frost when Úna closed the window for the night. It was a bitterly cold, starry night and an intense west wind was rattling the bedroom windows. She packed the fire with slack, removed her two overcoats from the coat rack in the hall and turned out the lights. In her bedroom, she removed her late husband's winter overcoat from her wardrobe, held it a moment and then went into the boys' bedroom. She placed the three overcoats over her sleeping sons and was about to leave the bedroom when she heard a voice.

'Is that you, Ma?' asked a sleepy Stephen.

'Go back to sleep,' she whispered. 'It's still night-time.'

'Ma, my legs feel funny again.'

Úna walked over to her son and placed her hand on his forehead.

'What do you mean your legs feel funny?'

'They're all tingly, will you rub them for me, Ma?'

Úna breathed on her hands and rubbed them together. She found the bottle of rubbing alcohol, pulled back the covers and messaged Stephen's legs.

'Is that better?'

'Yea, it feels lovely.'

'I thought you couldn't feel anything in your legs?'

'Well, I can now. Ma will you bend my legs?'

Úna lifted Stephen's legs to his chest and back down again.

'Do it again Ma.'

Úna repeated the action twice.

'Ma put my feet on the ground.'

'Are you sure? The floor is freezing.'

'Yea, do it.'

Úna lifted Stephen's legs out of the bed and placed his feet on the cold linoleum covered floor.

'I want to stand up,' Stephen said, his eyes almost shining in the dark. 'Help me up Ma, come on.'

Úna put her arm around her son and helped him to his feet.

'Do your legs still feel funny?'

'I don't know,' Stephen looked into his mother's face. 'Ma, let go of me.'

Úna moved slowly away from her son and he stood unsupported on his own.

'Move back, Ma.'

Úna took a step back. Stephen tried to lift his right leg but it didn't respond. He tried again, the same result. On the third attempt, his foot moved ever so slightly. Úna took a deep breath. Stephen tried again, slowly his right foot moved up and then forward. He put his weight on it and it held him. He moved his left leg forward and it too held his weight, he started to laugh and he slid to the floor. Úna rushed forward and caught her son in her arms and they both laughed and then cried.

'Ma, I can walk,' Stephen said. 'I can walk.'

'You can. Jesus, Mary and Joseph! You can walk. You are going to be alright.'

The following morning Stephen walked around the house, the following day he walked around the back garden, the day after that he walked up the Avenue and soon he was running and jumping and normal life returned to the Foley household.

CHAPTER 16
ANTO'S RAGE

Rain danced on the pavement in front of eleven-year-old Anto Ryan, the terror of the Avenue, as he huddled with his younger brother Sean in a Moore Street shop doorway. Soaked pedestrians carrying bags and baskets hurried past the boys. A street trader's hatchet pounded on her fish stall and the severed head of a mackerel leaped into the air, bounced off the stall and plopped at the feet of the younger boy.

'Ah,' cried Sean, staring at the dead eyes of the fish head.

'Don't worry son, he's well dead,' the dealer cackled, and with another swing of her hatchet another mackerel lost its head.

Anto put his arm around his brother. The Ryan boys were waiting on their mother, they knew she'd come, she always came but she wasn't always Ma, sometimes she was that other woman.

At last the door of Mooney's pub crashed open and there she was; hair dishevelled, face flushed with a cigarette dangling from her lips. Sean waved and she sauntered across the busy street. Anto was very good at reading his mother's moods and expressions. He could tell from the way she was breathing, how she looked at him or the sound of her footsteps, which of his two mothers was approaching: Ma or that other woman. Smelling of smoke and beer, she kissed her two sons. The anxious look in her eyes told him it wasn't Ma; it was the other woman.

'Are you going to be silly?' Sean asked when his mother slipped on a piece of fish-gut.

'Jasus, mind where you're dropping them things,' Ma yelled at the street trader.

'Ah, keep the head there, princess,' said the toothless trader.

Ma steadied herself against the shop window, her handbag fell open and Anto glimpsed the half-bottle of Jameson tucked into the bottom of the bag.

'We were waiting a long time for you Ma, what kept you?'

Ma ignored Anto's question, took Sean in her arms and rubbed his head a little too roughly.

'Your brother is a feckin moan, don't grow up like him. He takes after his da. Not your da, but his da,' Ma said, and laughed coarsely.

Anto hated Ma talking about his father as if he was nothing, but more than that, he hated when she mocked him in front of Sean. The rain beat down on the silent trio as they trudged up Moore Street, along Parnell Square and past the Plaza Cinema. When they reached the church the children called the Black Church, a rain-filled gust of wind whipped around the children's bare legs and blew Ma's umbrella inside out.

'Jasus,' she said, and threw the umbrella into the gutter. With their overcoats pulled over their heads, the family scurried past St Joseph's Convent School and on up Upper Wellington Street.

'It's chips to-night,' Ma said as the family stripped off their wet coats in the living room of Number Six. Sean was delighted, but Anto knew chips meant they had to go to bed early.

'Are those people coming again tonight?' Anto asked.

'Yes. I have a few friends dropping around for a little Christmas celebration, what's wrong with that?'

'Is that why you bought the bottle of whiskey?'

Ma lashed out and slapped Anto across the face. The sudden sharp shock of the blow paralysed him; he stared at his mother and she stuck her face into his.

'Do you begrudge me a Christmas drink with me friends. I work bloody hard. I look after you and your brother. I put clothes on your back, food in your stomach and shoes on your feet, not every kid in Dublin can say that.'

She slapped a shilling into Anto's hand. 'It's stopped raining, go to Marco's and get the feckin' chips. And be quick about it.'

As Anto pulled on his wet coat again, Ma yelled at him from the kitchen, 'And keep away from Pat Colgan. Go the long way to the chipper.'

But Anto didn't go the long way. Why should he? He wasn't afraid of Pat Colgan or anyone else. He crossed the street that divided the two Wellington Streets and was walking past a dark tenement doorway when a lighted cigarette butt flicked out of the darkness and bounced off his arm.

'Mind what you're doing, you bleeden eejit,' Anto screeched into the darkness of the doorway.

'Who are you calling an eejit,' the familiar voice said, as the lanky frame of fourteen-year-old Pat Colgan emerged into the light and expelled a lungful of smoke into Anto's face. Anto pushed him away. Caught off guard, Pat stumbled and Anto bolted down the street.

Pat gave pursuit.

'Pat Colgan! Where do you think you're going?' a voice bellowed from a window at the top of the tenement building. 'Get your bloody skinny arse up here, right now. I want you to do something for me.'

The fourteen-year-old stopped running. The one person in the world Pat Colgan didn't disobey was his step dad. Fuming, the lanky lad spat on the ground and shuffled back into the darkness of the tenement.

With two bags of hot chips under his arm, Anto stuck his head out of the door of Marco's chipper. All was clear, no Pat Colgan, but to be on the safe side, he decided to take the long way home. He ran down Dorset Street and when he got to the Black Church, he stopped. The street was deserted. Heart pounding he ran by the church and only stopped again to catch his breath when he reached the porch of St Joseph's Convent School. He was only a few seconds there when he heard hurrying footsteps. He looked about and saw Pat Colgan charging at him. His face exploded in pain; blood spurted out of his nose and gushed through his fingers. He stumbled backwards and the lanky fourteen-year-old kicked him, grabbed the bag of chips, tore it open and empted the steaming chips over Anto.

'What is going on down there?' Sister Fatima asked, popping her head out a window of the convent.

Pat grabbed Anto by his jacket's lapel.

'Gab on me and I'll get your feckin' brother.'

'Jesus, Mary and Joseph,' Ma said when she saw her son's bleeding face. 'What am I going to do with you? You're like your father, always fighting and getting into trouble. Look at you, look at your lovely face.'

Anto's mother walked him into the kitchen, stood him in front of the sink and washed his face in cold water. The boy stood in silence and watched the water turn red, swirl around the sink and then disappear down the drain.

'That's going to be sore for a few days, but I don't think anything is broken,' Ma said peering at Anto's nose. 'I haven't any more money, so we won't be having chips tonight.'

After a meal of bread smeared with dripping and some mugs of tea, Anto and Sean were sent to bed. Lying in the bed Anto's nose throbbed, his head and ankle ached and he had to breathe through his mouth. Ma sat on his bed; she placed a wet cloth on his nose and forehead and he felt a little better.

Mother had that dress on that made her look lumpy and she had stuff on her lips that made them look really red. She looked from Anto to Sean.

'Boys, I want yous to be quiet tonight, no loud talking. Do you hear me?'

Anto tucked his knees tight-up against his body and listened to the sounds of the house, he heard the swish of the curtains against the window, the whirl of air passing under the door and the creaking of the house. He heard the front door open and listened to his mother greet her so-called friends. He hated them all, Hairy Harry and his smelly mate Peter and Peter's ugly girlfriend Gene. He heard them talking, laughing and drinking. He knew soon enough they'd be arguing and shouting or singing. But what he hated most was they'd talk about him and his brother.

'Why don't you get rid of them kids of yours, you could do well for yourself,' Harry would say. 'A good-looking woman like you could have your pick of men.'

'I'm doing alright,' Ma would reply. Then they'd laugh the laugh of people who didn't give a toss for each other. Later when all the goodbyes were said and the hall door closed for the last time that night, Anto's rage calmed. When Ma's bedroom door closed, he looked around the near darkness and the demons of nothingness came and tormented him. But somewhere in among the torments of his thoughts, he remembered the one moment of the day when he had felt happy. It was when his mother placed the wet cloth over his nose, called him Anthony and told him everything was going to be alright. The pain in his head dulled and he drifted into sleep.

CHAPTER 17
CHRISTMAS 1950

Tadhg Mulligan buys a present

On Christmas Eve, nine months after his release from prison, Tadhg Mulligan walked into a chaotically busy Cleary's Department Store. People were rushing about, carrying bags filled with packages, shop assistants were pulling merchandise out of boxes and presenting them to customers and Bing Crosby was singing White Christmas over the public address system. A conflicted and confused Tadhg stood amid the bedlam and wondered what kind of present he should buy Lily Rattigan. She had invited him for Christmas dinner, he had accepted the invitation and now he had to get her a present.

'Are you alright Mr Mulligan?' asked a well-built man with a beautifully groomed beard and a Cork accent. 'I'm Eamon Flynn and I live in Number Twenty One on the Avenue, the house with the yellow door.'

'Hello Eamon, to tell you the truth, I'm a bit stuck. I have to buy a present for a friend and I don't know what to get.'

'I know how you feel. I've just bought my wife's present and I don't mind telling you, it's a great weight off my mind.'

'Could you advise me of what kind of present I should get my friend?'

'Well, that depends on what kind of a friend you're talking about.'

'You might know her, its Lilly Rattigan.'

'Indeed I do know Lily. I tell you how I solve my Christmas present problem, every year I give my Bridy a new cardigan and she always loves it. It's a great present and if it's not the right colour or size, sure, she can exchange it.'

'A cardigan, but I wouldn't know what class of a cardigan to buy.'

'I have the answer to that question too. Do you see that woman behind the cardigan counter? She's my sister Agnes. She'll put you right.'

Tadhg approached Mr Flynn's sister and after much consideration and conversation, he bought a hand-knitted, white Aran cardigan and when the woman offered to gift wrap it, he thought all his prayers had been answered.

The Ryan house – a visitor

It was late on Christmas Eve and Millie Ryan was putting the last few decorations on the Christmas cake when she heard young George screech. Next she heard her husband exclaim, 'My God!'

She rushed into the living room and there was her eldest son Tim. She burst into tears.

'I'm home for Christmas,' Tim said smiling broadly. 'I don't have to be back in England for a week.'

'Wonderful,' his mother said, and folded her arms around him.

'This is going to be a wonderful Christmas,' Mr Ryan said, and gripped his youngest son George's shoulder.

'He's not getting his old bed back,' said George.

'I don't think he cares about the bed,' said Mr Ryan. 'He's just happy to be home.'

The Foley House – preparing for Santa

On Christmas Eve, when all her guests had gone home, Úna Foley removed one of her precious cut-glass sherry glasses from the glass cabinet and poured herself a sweet sherry. Sitting by the dying fire, she spent the next hour packing toys and treats into three of her old nylon stockings. She put the latest Dandy comic, a packet of plastic soldiers, a flashlight and a box of Smarties into Joseph's stocking. A Beano comic, some Marla, a potato gun and a packet of fruit Pastilles into Stephen's stocking and a Film Fun comic, a magnifying glass, a science fiction novel and a fizz bag were stuffed into Peter's stocking. She pinned a lucky bag to the top of each stocking and tip-toed up the stairs to the boys' bedroom. She placed Peter's bulging stocking at the foot of his bed and was looking for the empty stocking he had placed there earlier when she heard a little voice.

'Is that you, Santa?'

'No, it's not,' Úna said, and placed the two other stockings on the end of the bed. 'Go back to sleep Stephen, Santa hasn't arrived yet.'

'I can't sleep. I'm too excited.'

'Everyone gets excited at Christmas,' Úna said taking the boy's hand and rubbing it.

'Does Santa come to big people?'

'Not really.'

'Don't worry, Ma, I bought you a present and Joseph made you a present and Peter has a present for you too. So you'll get lots of presents.'

'Well that's wonderful,' Úna said and held the boy's hand until he fell asleep again.

The Farrell House – Santa arrives

On Christmas morning at six o'clock young Molly Farrell awoke, felt a weight on her feet and wondered what it was. She looked across to her brother Johnny's bed but all she could see was darkness. Half frightened and half excited she slipped into her brother's bed.

'Wake up, Johnny, wake up.'

Johnny lifted his head off the pillow.

'What?'

'I think Santa was here.'

'Santa,' repeated Johnny sitting up. 'What did you get?'

'I didn't look.'

'Why not?'

'I'm afraid.'

'Jeepers the lino is freezing,' Johnny said when his feet touched the floor. He dashed across the bedroom and flicked on the light. When Molly saw the bulging Christmas stocking at the end of her bed her heart pounded. She dived across her bed and pulled the toys out of the stocking.

'Look, it's a comic book and a crying doll and lots of honey bee sweets,' Molly said unwrapping a honey bee and popping it into her mouth.

'Stop talking in there, put that light out and go back to sleep,' cried Mr Farrell from his bedroom.

'Da, Ma, Santa left us lots of toys,' Molly said as she rushed into her parent's bedroom and climbed in between them.

'Have you any idea what time it is? Go back to bed and come back at eight,' said a sleepy Mr Farrell

'Da, Ma, look I got a Chuck Connors Rifleman rifle, an annual and a bag of sweets,' Johnny said as he too joined his parents in their bed.

Victoria and Henrietta Lyons's Christmas – a brooch and a hope
After singing the Gloria hymn on Christmas morning in the pro-Cathedral, Victoria Lyons returned home and enjoyed breakfast

with her mother. After their meal they exchanged gifts and as they sat in front of a roaring fire Victoria again admired the beautiful brooch her father had sent her for Christmas. Henrietta looked into the fire and thought about the suitable young man she had arranged for Victoria to meet in the New Year.

Aiden Sweeny's Christmas – a surprise for Mother
Coincidently, after singing Gloria hymn in St Joseph's Church choir, Aiden Sweeny arrived home in great spirits. Mrs Sweeny was in the parlour arranging the Christmas presents neatly underneath the tree when the clock on the mantelpiece chimed two. Mr Sweeny turned on the fairy lights on the Christmas tree and placed the new Johnny Mathis Christmas LP on the record player. Then the family sat and enjoyed a most beautiful meal of spicy beef, braised celery and creamed potatoes. After desert Aiden left the house and an hour later returned with his new girlfriend, Roisin Murphy. Mrs Sweeny liked Roisin and talked to her all day. When Roisin was leaving and Aiden went to fetch her coat, Mrs Sweeny made Roisin promise to visit her, soon.

Mr Dunnock's Christmas – a late arrival
Freddy Dunnock was a little nervous, it was five past one and his guest had not arrived. The goose was cooked, the roast potatoes were ready and the sprouts were sitting in the pot stewing.

'She's late,' Freddy Dunnock said, as he rearranged the wine glasses on the table.

'Five minutes is not late,' Aunt Gertrude said as she poked the blazing fire in the living room. 'And stop fussing.'

Freddy disappeared into the kitchen and was opening the jar of port sauce he had bought in Finlaters when he heard the knock on the front door. He froze.

'I think your guest has arrived,' Aunt Gertrude called out.

Mr Dunnock walked through the living room, glanced momentarily at the Christmas tree, adjusted a bauble and walked down the newly-painted hallway.

'Ah, Maureen,' he said when he swung open the door. 'Come in, you're very welcome.'

'Sorry I'm late.'

'Are you? I hadn't noticed,' said Freddy.

Maureen glanced around the beautifully-decorated living room. 'The room is lovely; you certainly have an eye for decorating.'

'Thank you, I enjoy doing it, Christmas is a special time of year. It is good to make an effort, don't you think?'

'Yes I do, I certainly do.'

'Maureen, you know my Aunt Gertrude.'

'Of course, we met at Easter. How are you, Gertrude?'

'I am well, thank you. It's wonderful to see you again, Maureen, this nephew of mine has been telling me all the places you've been to together.'

Maureen smiled, Freddy opened a chilled bottle of Chablis and they enjoyed a most wonderful meal and over mince pies and brandy butter, they exchanged gifts.

Archie and Rachel's Christmas – another box of chocolates

The smell of cooking permeated the house and Archie's tummy ached with hunger. When the feast was ready Rachel brought the turkey, ham, stuffing, baked sprouts and roast potatoes to the perfectly set table. Archie eagerly carved the turkey and ham. After their meal he presented his wife with a beautiful necklace and, charmed and delighted with it, she had him fasten it around her neck.

'It's beautiful Archie,' Rachel kept repeating as she looked at herself in the living room mirror. 'It's really beautiful.'

Archie donned his coat, crossed the Avenue, knocked on the door of his neighbour's house and presented her with a full box of Fullers' chocolates.

Mrs Flynn's gifts – the greatest gift

The Flynn family exchanged gifts. Eamon was delighted with the striped shirt Bridy gave him but she was not pleased with yet another cardigan from her husband. Not wanting to hurt his feelings, she pretended to be delighted. Before baby Sean was put to bed for the night Eamon and his daughter Anne disappeared into the parlour, arranged the four special pillows on the sofa and placed baby Sean in the centre of them. Eamon returned to the kitchen, escorted his wife into the parlour and handed each member of the family a glass of lemonade and proposed a toast.

'Last Christmas we were a family of three and this Christmas, because of my lovely daughter and my equally beautiful and smart wife, we are now four. I am so happy that we have a new member of our family and I'm sure he is going to bring us great joy and many blessings. Let's lift our glasses to baby Sean.'

The Canon's Christmas – alone

Christmas day was always a very lonely day for Canon Breathnach. Every Christmas he gave his housekeeper two days off to visit her family in Waterford. Like any good housekeeper, Mrs Keane had prepared meals for the Canon, all he had to do was remove the greaseproof paper wrapping and place them in the oven to warm them up. The Canon had received more than a few invitations for Christmas dinner from parishioners, but he felt the invitations were offered more out of a sense of duty or worse, pity, rather than a sincere desire to share his company. After all religious services were over and the church was locked up, the Canon sat by the fire in his house in Geraldine Street, opened a bottle of Jameson and hoped he wouldn't finish it before bedtime. Father Hannan, sitting alone in his house a few streets away, was wondering if he should have a second glass of whiskey.

Denis William's Christmas – a little surprise

On the afternoon of Christmas day, Denis Williams knocked on the door of Mrs Kenny's flat in Wellington Street. When the woman pulled open the door he handed her a large brown paper parcel.

'What is this?' asked the astonished woman.

'Mrs Drake, the woman who gave Darragh the clothes for his Communion asked me to give you this parcel. She said there are a few clothes in there you might like and a few things for Darragh. How is your boy?'

'He's not too bad, he's having a little rest. He was disappointed Santa didn't bring him any presents, but I hadn't a penny. Thank you for the parcel, tell Mrs Drake I'm much obliged and tell her I'll say a prayer for her.'

'I certainly will, but there is one other thing.' Smiling, Denis leaned down and picked up a brown paper-covered box. 'This is for Darragh, it's a wind-up train set and tracks. You can tell him that Santa came when he was resting.'

The woman's eyes started to glisten.

'I will, I will. The blessings of God on you sir, thank you very much. I can't wait until he wakes up.'

'Mammy, who's at the door,' said a little voice in the flat.

'You look after yourself,' Denis said and touched the rim of his new trilby hat.

'Darragh, you're not going to believe who just came to the door.'

Denis walked down the stairs and he did something he hadn't done in years, he whistled.

The Foleys again, this time for a game of cards and a glass of sherry

On Christmas Day afternoon, Uncle Martin made his customary Christmas visit to the Foley household. Upon arrival, he gave each child ten pennies, produced a deck of cards and everyone played cards for money. Somehow every year, Uncle Martin managed to lose his money. However, if any of the boys lost their money he'd slip them another few pennies. At five thirty, Jacinta arrived with an iced Christmas cake. Úna made tea and everyone had a slice of cake. When Martin left and the children were asleep, Úna and Jacinta sat by the fire and enjoyed a lovely glass or two of Sandeman's sherry.

End of Day with the Farrells
Mrs Farrell put Johnny and Molly to bed. She kissed each child, said goodnight and as she put out the light, young Johnny said, 'Ma that was the best Christmas, ever.'

ACKNOWLEDGMENTS

They say it takes a village to raise a child, the same can almost be said about writing a book. Many people have contributed to the creation of this book and to each of them I give my thanks for their support, advice and encouragement.

Thanks to all the people of The Avenue who are the heart of these stories. While most of the stories were inspired by real persons, all of the characters and events described in the book are completely fictional.

I would like to thank my early readers of the developing manuscript; Mary and Joe Brennan, Ann O'Reilly and in particular Angela Lawton whose willingness to critique with reckless abandon was not just admirable, but also very helpful. I hope the experienced was not too traumatic for any of you.

I am greatly indebted to Helen Falkner and David O'Flaherty for their expert, insightful and clear editing of the book. Many thanks to my eagle eyed proof-reader George Brust for his thorough and diligent work and whose insightful notes are almost worth publishing themselves. Any lingering mistakes and discrepancies are mine.

My thanks to Godfrey Smeaton for his atmospheric watercolour painting used for the book's cover. Thanks to Brendan Beirne for the book cover design and for his generosity in sharing his knowledge and insight into Irish life.

Very special thanks to my family, Paul, Therese, Chloe, Jamie, Mark, Maeve and my new granddaughter Molly, for their endless interest in the developing book. Perhaps Molly didn't have all that much interest but who knows.

Finally nobody deserves more thanks and credit than my wife Julie, her endless patience and ongoing support during the writing of this labour of love was vital and endless.

This book is available as a paperback and an e-book from
Amazon.com
You can e-mail me at
cecilallen93seapark@gmail.com

If you enjoyed 'The Avenue' you might like to read Cecil Allen's
other books
'The Actor –A Novel' and 'Constructing Alice.'

THE ACTOR – A NOVEL

Cecil Allen

A story of love and passion set in a time of war and violence.
A story of one man's struggle to find his place in the world.
A story of theatre.
A story of life.

The Actor is a page turner, full of colourful characters, wit, tragedy and humour.

In 1914 a young Jim Brevin runs away from his comfortable, middle-class Dublin home and joins a theatrical fit-up company travelling around Ireland.

On the day he becomes an apprentice with the famous *Ira Allen's Company of Irish Players* he reluctantly gets involved in The Rising.

He is mistaken for a spy, marries a rebel's sister, discovers fraud and theft in the family business and suffers a horrendous personal tragedy. In time he becomes a celebrated actor and at the moment of his greatest theatrical success he is faced with a stark choice.

Praise for 'The Actor – A Novel'
'A powerful, touching thoroughly absorbing novel.'
'I loved the story, the characters and the effortless imagery.'
'Very descriptive, very atmospheric, a great book.'
'I was brought to tears many times.'
'An excellent read, vivid and entertaining.'

Available as a paperback and an e-book from Amazon.com

CONSTRUCTING ALICE

Cecil Allen
*We do not control our lives but
neither does chance.*

To the casual observer Alice Dalton's life might have seemed idyllic. But in the quiet of her middle class Dublin home she lived her life with a damaged mother, an authoritarian father, rebellious brothers and warring sisters.

In a bitterly deeply divided country that is tearing itself apart, Alice's pursuit of independence, identity and love takes her on a perilous journey through attraction, betrayal, intolerance, hypocrisy and duplicity.

Praise for 'Constructing *Alice*'
It's a real page-turner – I just couldn't put it down –such a vivid picture of Dublin in the early 20th century, it was just like being there!
— Mary Clarke, Theatre Archivist Dublin City Library

A deeply moving love story.'
— Northside News.

'Five stars, exceptional both heartbreaking and uplifting.
— Amazon UK.

An extraordinary novel...bright, memorable and powerful.
— Frank West, Irish American News

Available as a paperback and an e-book from Amazon.com